Bob Moats

Kennel Murders

1

Kennel Murders

For information and address:
Magic 1 Productions
P.O. Box 524, Fraser MI 48026-0524
Website: http://murdernovels.com
Cover by Bob Moats

Bob Moats

Other Jim Richards series books by Bob Moats

For a preview or to purchase a book, go to
http://murdernovels.com

What a few people are saying about Murder Novels by Bob Moats

Mr. Moats, I just got your novel "Classmate Murders" and have to let you know, I read it in one evening. That is the first book I have ever done that with. That was the most enjoyable book I have ever read. I just started reading e-books, and reading again, after getting my wife a Kindle. This book was my 12th, and the best. I just got Las Vegas Showgirls to (read) tomorrow evening. I look forward to reading many of your books in this series. I have been searching for an author and books that were fun, entertaining reads. Your books are just the ticket.

Regards, A new fan, Bill from South Carolina

****

Another very nice comment submitted through my website from Micki P.:

"I recently was given a kindle for my 60th birthday. The first book I downloaded was the Classmate Murders and have now read every one of the them. Today I started on the Fatal Rejection series. Thank you for the wonderful ride with Jim and Penny and all the rest of the troop. I have laughed and giggled thru the stories, my poor family gave me the strangest looks! Now I really want a little Yorkie!! Fatal Rejection so far is another great read! I will be looking out for more of Jim Richards and since you are my #1 Author, anything of yours I can find."

Extra special thanks to:

Special thanks to Val Brooks who edited this book and for her great suggestions.

Thanks to the beta readers Cindy Gross Valstad, Susan Houghton and Al Norris.

Thank you to all the people who purchased this book. I hope you enjoy it as much as I enjoyed writing it for my faithful readers.

The Jim Richards Family of Readers is listed in the back of the book.

Kennel Murders by Bob Moats

Chapter 1

It was a yap fest in the dark room as the two men walked among the cages of excited dogs. They had flashlights and were examining the cards on the cages, looking for certain canines. The fancier the breed, the better. After a half hour, they had what they wanted and took the large box out to their van. They slid the box into the back and drove off. In the morning, the kennel employees would realize they had been robbed.

~~*~~

When people get to a certain age, they shouldn't be doing anything dangerous to their health. Okay, in all fairness, I was in a dangerous business. My private investigating firm had its share of dangerous cases, especially when it came to murder. I have this curse, murder seems to follows me. Or, so my wife keeps telling me. But I'm getting away from the point. I get involved in dangerous activities, and this was one of them.

No, not murder or any such thing that would glorify my situation. Here's what happened. I brought out the ladder from the garage and proceeded to try and change the spotlight on the corner of the house, the one that lights the driveway at night. I really should have had someone hold the ladder for me, but I'm a careful person. Or so I thought.

I was only about five feet off the ground when I turned the wrong way and my foot missed the step. I came down on my left leg and just knew something was wrong when I felt, and heard, the cracking sound from my lower leg. I also knew when I couldn't stand that something was terribly wrong.

Penny, my wife and famous talk show host, was out by the pool. The noise from our ugly Greek statue pouring water into the koi pond was just loud enough to cover my cries for help. I pulled my cell phone out and dialed her. Luckily, she had her phone by the pool with her.

"Hello? Are you getting too lazy to come talk to me in person?" she said before I had a chance to talk. She did that a lot.

"Okay, dispense with the pleasantries, I need help out front. It seems I broke my leg and I could use you out here now." I replied.

"Are you in pain?"

"Well, if you broke your leg, wouldn't you be in pain?"

"Okay, I'll be right there. Should I call an ambulance?"

"I'm not sure yet. Just come see if you can help me up and I'll decide."

I heard her hang up and I waited. Shortly, she came around the side of the house and over to me on my back, flat out on the ground.

"Sweetie, are you all right?" she asked.

"I doubt it seriously. Help me to stand and I'll see if I need an EMS unit."

She helped me to sit, then tried to bring me up to my feet. As soon as I put weight on my left leg, I went down again. The pain was worse than when I fell the first time. I hated pain, so I gasped for her to call for help.

She dialed 911, and then called my office to see if Buck was in. He was, so she told him what happened and he said he'd be right out.

I'm sure Buck broke a lot of traffic laws, because he arrived before the ambulance.

"Damn, Jim, you should know better than to climb a ladder without someone to help," he said, half grinning. "You could have called me."

"I didn't want to disturb anyone. My vacation is getting boring and all I've done is odd jobs around the house."

We heard the EMS unit roaring up the street, sirens blaring. I was pretty much known by the medical teams as they have been to my house numerous times to patch up criminals. They pulled into the drive and came over to me.

"Mr. Richards, you aren't supposed to be the one hurt," one med tech said.

"It was a dangerous criminal who attacked me then ran off."

They looked at the ladder still standing and grinned.

"Got to watch out for those dangerous criminal ladders," the other tech said as they studied my leg.

I winced in pain as they probed and pulled. "Yep, it looks broken," one man said and they brought out the inflatable splint and put it around my leg. Then they brought out the gurney and carefully put me on it.

I looked at Penny and said, "If I don't make it, give everything I own to charity."

She smiled and said, "Like hell, I'll sell it all and go on a cruise."

"You are so caring," I said, as they put me in the van.

Buck yelled, "I'll bring Penny to the hospital after she changes. Anyone you want me to call?"

"Yeah, my lawyer. I'm going to sue the ladder." The tech closed the door.

I was looking at the ceiling of the EMS unit and wondering how long I was going to be out of commission. We arrived at the hospital and they wheeled me into the ER. I spent the next two hours being poked, probed, and x-rayed enough to tell me what I already knew. I had a broken leg.

I found Penny and Buck waiting in the private room I requested after the nurse brought me back from having my leg plastered. They set the leg back in place and said I'd probably be in the cast for a while. They weren't being time specific, seeing as I was an "older" person, my bones may not heal as fast. But they said I'd be up and around on crutches.

"Damn, this messes up my vacation," I said to Penny.

"Jim, the whole point of you taking time off was to do some work around the house. Which you've neglected since we moved in. Now you have an excuse to not do anymore work."

"I can hire someone to do all that stuff," I said.

"Should have thought of that before you climbed the ladder," Buck said from his chair by the bed.

"Thanks for the afterthought. How's the office doing?"

"Earl and Trapper are busy on domestic cases and Lynn is off tracking down a missing person who came to Vegas to gamble. Probably lost his shirt and is hiding downtown in a bar. I've got nothing right now, so I can help you get around."

Kennel Murders

"Thanks Buck. I appreciate it. The doctor said I could leave tomorrow after they get me up and walking with crutches."

"I'll have to go to work at the studio, so you'll have to fend on your own around the house," Penny said.

Buck said, "I'll come over to baby sit him in the morning."

"Will you make my toast and take me out for a walk?" I asked him.

"Do you want me to bathe you, too?" he said with his famous walrus grin.

"I don't think that will be necessary. A sponge bath would be nice though. Penny, you could dress like a nurse and sponge bathe me."

"Ha! Buck can dress like a nurse and take care of it." Penny said.

"I'm not shaving my legs to dress like a nurse. No sponge baths from me. You can do that for yourself," he said with a smirk now.

Penny kissed my forehead and said she had to go in early tomorrow to her studio. "We're having a show about the big dog competition this week at the MGM Grand arena. The studio will have lots of dogs and I want to get settled with them. I'll take Willy with me, to show him off."

"He'd win all the prizes, I'm sure. Lot of fancy breeds in the show?"

"Yep, all future winners in their categories," Penny said.

"Reminds me of the time I had to act as bodyguard for that dog in the dog show back in Michigan." Buck said.

"I'm sure it will be the same thing. But no killer sons to worry about," Penny said as she got ready to leave with Buck. "See you tomorrow, sweetie." She kissed me again and they left.

I turned on the TV I requested for the room, put the bed up in a sitting position, and thought, this wasn't too bad.

*

Chapter 2

I was falling off the Stratosphere Tower in Vegas. I watched myself getting closer to the ground and at the last minute, I put my feet down to stop my fall. I came to an abrupt halt, then my legs started to crumple and my body was on the ground. I woke to find the nurse standing by my bed trying to wake me.

"Mr. Richards, you were having a bad dream. Are you alright now?" she asked.

I was sweating and she dabbed my head with a towel.

"It's bad enough to fall from half-way up a ten foot ladder, but not good to fall off the Stratosphere Tower," I said, calming now.

"No, not good to fall from there." She smiled. "If you need anything, let me know. Just push the call button," she said and left the room.

The sun was peeking through the window and I could see it was going to be another hot, sunny day. I just rested until a large male nurse came in with a pair of crutches. He proceeded to get me out of bed and had me do a walk around on the crutches. It wasn't easy, but I managed. I didn't like it.

"Very good, Mr. Richards. You'll do fine getting around," he said, helping me back in bed. "I really enjoy your books."

"Thank you. I appreciate it. How long before I can leave?"

"Well, you did well with the crutches. We didn't want to turn you out without trying them. I'd say you can leave today. We only kept you to make sure you were alright."

I was sure because of my age, they were afraid I'd fall on my face. "Good, I'll call my wife and let her know."

He left the room and I picked up my cell phone from the bedside table and called Penny. It was early enough that she was probably still home. The phone rang a few times then she answered. "Penny's Dog Rescue Agency." She answered.

I could hear lots of barking in the background, and then remembered she was going in to her studio early to see the dogs. "How's the mutts?"

"It's crazy here. I'm glad I came in early so I know what to expect. Are they letting you out today?"

"That's what the nurse said who brought my crutches."

"Was the nurse cute?" Penny asked.

"Nope, she hadn't trimmed her beard, so I wasn't attracted." I heard silence then I said, "It was a male nurse, so don't worry I won't run off with him."

"You better not. Has Buck gotten there yet?"

"I haven't seen him. But it's still early."

"I have to go, Gordy just came in with a couple suits and he's waving to me."

"Okay, see you later," I said and hung up.

I flipped on the TV and waited for Buck to show up. After a while, I could hear his voice in the hallway talking to the nurses. Fine, I'm crippled and he's flirting. I waited, and then he finally popped in.

"Did you get a date with any of them?" I asked.

"Huh?"

"The nurses, I could hear you out there talking them up."

"Oh, them, no. They're nice but not my style."

"You have a style? Blond, built, and dumb?"

"I'm not that crass. I like intellectual women, too. Then blond and well built."

"You wouldn't turn down a brunette, or a red-head?"

"I like all the ladies," he said, showing his big walrus smile. If he ever shaved his mustache, he'd lose that smile. "Are you ready to go?"

"If I can leave."

"The nurse said for me to get you out of here. So get up and let's go."

The same male nurse brought in a wheel chair and said I had to leave the hospital that way.

"So I can't injure myself on the way out and sue?" I said.

"Something like that. Once we take you out to the curb, you can break anything you want," he said with a grin.

Kennel Murders

I was wheeled out after signing some release papers, and Buck took me down to the new van I had bought for the firm. He opened the side door and I saw a nice, shiny, chrome wheelchair.

"You got me my own wheelchair?" I asked.

"Yep, and it's motorized. I took it for a spin at the medical store. I'll soup it up for you."

I laughed and said, "You'll have to take it out of the van since we don't have a lift."

"No problem." He helped me to stand and the male nurse took the hospital's wheelchair back after saying his good-byes. Buck helped me into the passenger side of the van. I had trouble with the cast fitting in the front seat leg space, so he helped me into the wheelchair in the back.

"Home, sir," I said.

When we got to the house, he looked at the side of the van and said, "I can get one of those portable ramps so we can wheel you down. I'll run over to get one after I get you settled in the house."

"I can get around with the crutches," I said.

"Jim, years ago I broke a leg falling off my motorcycle. Pretty much the same injury as you have. I tried to get around on the crutches and it was miserable. Take my advice and use the wheelchair I got you."

I agreed and he carefully brought the chair down out of the van. I knew a ramp would help getting me in and out, so I'd let him get one. Besides, it could come in handy other times. He wheeled me into the house and parked me in the living room.

He handed me the TV remote and said, "Now, don't get into any trouble before I get back."

He left me to try the wheelchair's driving abilities. It was fun actually. I may enjoy this. My cellphone buzzed and I reached into the pocket of the robe Buck brought for me. I couldn't get my pants over the cast, so I had to wear a robe.

"Hello?" I answered. The caller ID showed private. I didn't like answering those calls, but I was lonely at the moment, and I wanted someone to talk to. Even a telemarketer.

The voice on the phone asked for Jim Richards. "That's me, can I help you?"

The voice continued, "I got your number from a police detective named Williams. I need your help."

So the police hadn't heard about my predicament yet. "What is it you need?"

Kennel Murders

"I own a dog kennel and late last night someone broke in and stole four of our dogs. They were expensive breeds and the owners are not happy. I called the police, but they have too many cases to worry about dognappers right now. The detective gave me your number and said you could help."

"How expensive are these dogs and is there a call for a ransom?"

"The dogs are worth a great deal. They're show dogs and can bring a great deal of money for breeding services. I told the owners I would take care of finding the criminals. I have no idea how to do that. Can you help?"

"I'm out of my office right now. Can you come in this afternoon?"

"I'll be there."

I gave her directions to my office and hung up. Now, I would have to figure how to get dressed.

Buck came back a short time later and had the ramp. I told him about the case and he said it sounded like the one back in Michigan.

"Yes, but that dog wasn't kidnapped. He was threatened with harm. I've never come across dogs being taken for ransom."

"Was there a ransom call made?"

"Not yet, but I'm sure this is the reason for the theft. Expensive dogs, potential money to be made. Has to be the reason. Now, I need to get to the office."

"You need to get some pants," Buck said with a laugh.

"Go in my dresser, there is a pair of jogging pants. They have snaps up the side and should work to cover me." Buck got the pants and we struggled to put them on, but it worked. I was covered.

I drove out to the van. Luckily, the house was handicapped accessible from a previous owner. I got to the van and Buck had the ramp attached to the open side. I rolled up and into the van. Buck was delighted.

"Shall we go?" I said.

*

Chapter 3

I rolled into the back door of my building. Luckily, it was level with the sidewalk so I could enter easily. I rolled down the hallway and stopped at Earl's office. He wasn't in. I wheeled over to Trapper's office, he was also gone. I hoped they were out working cases. Buck was following behind me. I presumed he was watching to see that I didn't drive into any walls.

I got to the glass doors to the front lobby, and Buck came around to help open them. I rolled over to Lacey's counter and found my head was lower than the counter top. I yelled, "Lacey!"

I heard a scream. Now I was startling her from below. Buck came up behind and pointed down to me. Lacey came to the counter and looked down.

"What happened to you?" she exclaimed, looking shocked.

"A little run in with an evil ladder. I have a woman coming in who wants to talk to me about a theft at a kennel. Send her to my office."

"How long are you going to be in the chair?" she asked.

"Actually, I like riding around in this. I may keep it up even after I heal. The doctors said it may be a while. Just until my bones mend."

"I'll have to get you one of those bicycle flags to put on the back of the chair, so I'll know where you are," Lacey said with a grin.

"Get one with a pirate skull and cross bones." Buck said.

I looked up at Buck and said, "I don't think so." He laughed.

"I'll see if I can get a handicapped license plate for the chair," Buck said.

The front entrance opened and in came a woman. I smiled and said, "Are you the kennel owner?"

She gave me a strange look sitting in my chair. "Yes, I am. Is Jim Richards in?"

"That's me. Forgive the chair, I had an accident yesterday. Would you follow me and my associate, Mr. Carson, into my office, please?" I looked at Buck and he opened the glass door as I wheeled in.

23

Kennel Murders

I hadn't been in my office yet, so I didn't have it ready for me in the wheelchair. Buck caught my concern and moved the desk chair away. I thanked him and wheeled around to my desk. Buck offered the woman a chair and then he sat on a chair on the side of the desk facing her.

"And you are?" I asked.

"Cindy Valstad. I own the Happy Puppy Boarding Kennel. Last night, someone broke in and took four show dogs that were very expensive. They left all the other dogs alone, so they must have known what animals to take."

"And you talked to the police?" I asked.

"Yes, they came out and filed a report, and they told me they would do their best to find the dogs. But, the police officer also said it would be a low priority due to the amount of other cases they had. Then he suggested I get a private investigator to help. There was a detective with them, named Williams, and he suggested you."

"I know Detective Williams. First, I'll need some information from you. As you see, I'm a little indisposed at the moment, but my associate, Mr. Carson, will be helping on this case."

Buck gave her a smile and I handed her a pad of paper and pencil to write down her info.

"Let me ask this, did any of the dogs have those ID chips under their skin?"

"They all did. But they are easy to remove with a little skill. Most valuable show dogs have the chips."

"Why were these dogs in your kennel if they were show dogs?"

"A lot of the owners can't have animals in their hotel or motel, so they have to board them. The owners don't like it, but not much they can do. Sometimes, they just smuggle the dog into their rooms, and hope not to get caught. This robbery could ruin my kennel's reputation. I hope you can solve this fast."

"We'll do our best, but I can't guarantee speedy results. We don't know what we are up against, yet."

"Well, whatever you can do, thank you." She handed the pad and pencil back. I looked at it and said it had everything we needed.

Buck finally spoke, "I'm going to come to your kennel to look over the place. Are you heading back there?"

"I am. I left my assistant watching the place. She may not be able to handle explaining to people about their missing dogs."

"Okay, if Jim is finished, I'll follow you over to your place." He stood and went to the door and waited.

"I have nothing more. You can give our secretary in front a retainer or we can bill you."

"Bill me, please. I just hope I don't get sued for the loss of the dogs." She stood, and Buck escorted her out.

I knew Buck could handle this without me, he was good at investigating. I was suddenly feeling helpless since he left. I guess I would have to suck it up and fend for myself. I wheeled out of my office and went to the front. I managed to open the glass doors and get out to the counter. I was singing "Row, row, row your boat," so Lacey knew I was coming.

"I hate that song, pick something else," Lacey yelled to me.

"What would you suggest?" I said, as I came to the side of the counter, where I could see her.

"Silence would be nice. Just cough when you come up here to the front."

"I can do that. Where is everyone?"

"Lynn is looking for a missing man. Trapper is tailing a bad husband, and Earl is trying to solve missing funds in an investment firm. You are here, and you are going to drive me crazy, aren't you?"

"Not if I can help it. I'm going to my office to meditate," I said and turned the chair back towards my office.

I heard Lacey say, "Have a nice sleep," as I went back through the doors. I wheeled into my office and sat wondering what to do now. This was going to drive me crazy. I hoped Penny would come in soon.

I looked at my watch, it was time for her to arrive, if she hadn't gotten involved in something else. I turned on the TV and watched her on her show talking to people with dogs. I turned up the volume and listened.

Penny was holding Willy in her arm and he was having a fit to get at the other dogs. He usually doesn't see other dogs very often. Maybe we'd have to get a playmate for him. Another toy Yorkie?

"And your name is?" Penny asked a woman holding two dogs on leashes.

"Linda Kennero, from Sweden, and these are my Jack Terriers, Morgana and Tristan.

"Beautiful dogs," Penny said and went to the next woman.

"I'm Nancy Davis, and this is Tico, my dachshund."

"Thank you and you are?" she asked the next woman in line.

"Erika Hale, and this is Sophie, my Jack Russell.

"Pretty dog, and you are?" She continued down the line.

"Karen Higham, this is my Cairn Terrier, Harvey."

She held her microphone to the next woman.

"I'm Leslie Jackson and this is Chloe, a toy Yorkie, like your dog.

Willy was really fussing now. A female toy Yorkie. Penny held him tightly.

"Well, Willy is getting too excited." Penny laughed and moved away from the women and their dogs.

"So, the All-Breeds Dog Show, sponsored by Wilson's Hearty Dog Chow, will be at the MGM Grand arena this weekend. This is not a sanctioned AKC event. It's for all dogs, of all breeds, to strut their stuff and maybe pick up a trophy."

"Now, I want to introduce a dog that served this country, and her owner, Deborah Sullivan." Penny went to a woman on the side and introduced her. "This is Leta, a Belgian Malinois, who is a retired military bomb dog. This is the first bomb dog I've met, even though I've met a lot of law enforcement, never a bomb sniffing dog. Thank you, Deb, for bring such a heroic dog here today."

Penny went to the front of her stage and closed the show. "I'll take Willy home and let him run loose, to take out his frustrations. Thanks for joining us today and see you tomorrow."

The show ended, and I almost jumped out of the chair when Penny said from my door, "So, what did you think?"

*

Chapter 4

"Very nice way to torment Willy," I said with a smile. "Did you let him play with the other dogs?"

"No, most of the dogs were bigger than he was. I was afraid one would take a bite and swallow him whole."

Penny put the dog down and he came bounding over to my chair. I reached down and picked him up. "Want to go for a ride, puppy?" Willy licked my hand.

"Nice chair. Where did you get it?" Penny asked.

"Buck got it this morning, and then he got a ramp for the van so I can be transported around."

"Well, don't expect me to be your chauffer. I'm not fond of driving the van. Where is Buck?"

"He's out on an assignment. Seems a kennel was broken into last night and four show dogs were taken. The owner hired us to find the dogs."

"The dogs must have something to do with the dog show this weekend. Why would they be taken?"

"I'm thinking ransom," I said. "They were valuable dogs, so the owners had to have money."

"Not necessarily. I met one woman in the beginning of the show, that you probably missed, and she wasn't rich. Just a woman with a show dog that was valuable. Her name was Susan Haughton and her dog, Ilse, is a show caliber Germen Shepherd. Susan sells homes and isn't rich. So not all owners have money."

"Well, I'm sure these people had money, they were boarding their dogs and staying at hotels that didn't allow animals. Most of the swanky expensive hotels in town don't like dogs pooping in their lobby."

"True, but would they have enough money to get their dogs back?"

"Maybe, but if someone took Willy, you'd pay any amount to get him back, right."

She grinned. "Yes I would, and then they'd have to face my Smith & Wesson."

"You have to stop shooting people. I'm surprised they didn't book you for shooting that hitman out in New York at the hotel last month," I said.

"He was a bad man and I did the courts a favor. Now, how good are you at getting around in that thing?"

I drove the chair out from behind my desk and came up to her.

"Of course, Buck got you a motorized wheelchair. You men and your toys. I have the feeling we won't be doing much together. I'm not going to be able to help you get around in that thing. Since you sent Buck off, he won't be able to help you either."

"That's alright. When Buck takes me home later, I'll just go into my home office and work on my books. I'm getting behind in my stories."

"Did you get rid of your publisher yet?"

"Since Morty is being investigated by the IRS for tax evasion, the company is in a holding pattern for now. I talked to Gino, and since he owns Lifton Publishing, I'm switching to them. I hope I get all my royalties this time."

"Wouldn't you be concerned that a publishing company owned by the mob would take a bigger cut of your royalties?"

"I have faith in Gino that he will take care of me. He offered me a very nice contract. Now, how do I get something to eat, I'm hungry?"

"You could roll down to Sonic and park the chair in one of their curb service spaces." Penny said with a smirk.

"You could stand on the back of the chair and go with me."

"Forget it. I'm taking Willy and going home to lavish around the pool. I need to get the dog smell off me." She took Willy from my lap and kissed me. "If Buck doesn't come back, I'll see you whenever." She went out, leaving me alone again.

I wheeled out to the lobby again and coughed as I entered Lacey's domain.

"Better, now what do you want?" lacey said.

"Food, call for a pizza and have it delivered to my office. Get a couple for everyone." I said. "Get the deluxe with everything but anchovies."

"I can do that. I don't think they even offer anchovies anymore."

"Whatever, just tell them to hurry. I haven't eaten today." I rolled back to my office and waited.

Kennel Murders

~~*~~

Buck wandered around the kennel examining the cages that had contained the stolen dogs.

"I don't suppose you ever lock the cages?" he asked Valstad.

"No, we didn't feel it was necessary. Even if we had, the locks could be broken," she said.

"True, how did they get in?"

She led him to a door at the back of the building and showed him where they forced it to get in.

"It wasn't a very good lock, we never figured anyone would break in," she said.

"I can recommend a good alarm security company that can install better doors and locks."

"Kind of like locking the barn door after the horses escaped," she said with a smile.

"Chances are you won't have this happen again. Law of averages. Like lightening striking twice in the same spot."

"Actually, that has happened. So I guess anything can happen. But I will be getting better protection for the building now."

"The police probably won't be breaking their schedule to find the dogs. I'll see what we can do. Do you have any security cameras out back where they parked?"

"We don't, but the party store next door has one. I don't know if it sees my back area."

"I'll go over and check. If you get any calls for ransom, call me immediately." He handed her his card and said, "I'll be in touch."

He went out the back door and over to the party store. He was hoping to find a camera in back, but didn't see one. The driveway from the back of the buildings went between them. Maybe the cameras in front caught the vehicle coming out. He went to the front door, in, and asked for the owner or manager.

"I'm the manager, can I help you?" A rather attractive woman said.

Buck handed her his card and said, "I'm investigating a robbery at the kennel next door and was wondering if your security cameras may have caught the vehicle leaving the area?"

"I'd love to help you but our cameras have been down for a couple days. The security company sent someone out the day before yesterday and said he had to order a part. I haven't heard from them since."

"Well, thanks for your time," Buck said and went out. He looked around and then saw the camera out front towards the top of the building. He went over to it and looked up. He saw what the real problem was. The coaxial cable had been cut. This was deliberate and probably caused by the dognappers.

Buck went back in and asked the woman, "Who is your security company?"

"Arcon Security. I've had them about a year now, why?"

"Did you put in a call for service on the camera?"

"No, they just came and said their monitors showed our camera was down. I didn't know we even had them watching."

"If they return, call me." Buck said and left again. He was going to check out Arcon Security now.

*

36

Chapter 5

Buck was standing at the counter of Arcon Security. It was a modest building by itself on Warm Springs Road just below the airport. Buck could tell they didn't have monitoring capabilities. They were in business to install security cameras and alarms and that was all.

An older man came out from the back and asked, "May I help you?"

Buck handed the man his card and said, "I'm investigating a robbery at a kennel and the party store next door had a camera installed by your company. It had its coaxial cable cut. Were you aware of this?"

"We don't know if any of our cameras are working or not until the owners calls, and then we go in and fix it."

"So, you didn't send someone to Lastrad Party Store to work on a camera?"

"Lastrad? I know them, but we haven't sent anyone to work on their system."

"Well, you need to go look at their camera. It's been disabled. Which gave cover to the robbery."

"That's not good. I'll have someone look into it, thank you."

Buck went back to the van and figured that the robbery was well planned. He got in and decided to go back to the office.

~~*~~

I finished the last of my pizza, or as much as I could eat. I know my eating habits weren't the best and I really needed to lose some weight. One thing I loved about Penny was that she accepted me as I was. Warts, big gut and all. That's love. She didn't bug me to lose weight and occasionally joked about me being her little Buddha.

I was hoping Buck would get back soon so I could go home. I wasn't going to like this imposition of being bound to the chair. Maybe I should give the crutches a try. They were just standing in my office, where Buck put them. I wheeled over and tried to stand by them. I ended up losing my balance, luckily I fell back into the chair. I decided it wasn't a good idea to try this alone.

I moved the chair back into the middle of the room and pulled my cell phone. I dialed Buck to see where he was at. He answered after the first ring.

"You all right, Jim?" he said right off.

"I'm fine, just wondering how you were doing."

"Good. I'm in the back parking lot. I'll be in shortly."

"Okay, talk soon," I said and hung up. Great, now I can get out of here.

He came in, I wondered how he got in without setting off Lacey's cowbell alarm, and told me about what he found.

"I agree. The camera being disabled had to be the work of the criminals. There's no other leads?"

"Nope, I haven't found out if they had CSI dust the place for prints, but I doubt they even called forensics to come in. I get the feeling this wasn't high on their priority."

"All we can do now is wait and see what their next move is." I said.

"I'm hoping the perps aren't shipping the dogs to some puppy mill. I saw that on TV. They steal dogs and sell them to pet shops and get decent money." Buck said.

"These are show dogs, people who own pet shops may question where the dogs came from. I hope."

"Well, we just wait then. Are you ready to go home?"

"You bet. There's pizza in the break room if you want to eat before you take me home."

"That sounds like a winner. Be right back." Buck left me alone again. I turned the chair to the door and wheeled out. I saw Earl's office light was on so drove there.

He was at his desk doing paperwork. I sat just outside his door until he looked over to me.

"Jim, geez, what happened to you?" he said, standing and coming around his desk to me.

"I had an accident yesterday with a mean ladder. I'm surprised Lacey hasn't told you."

"I haven't been up there yet. I snuck in the back and I'm getting my report finished before she badgers me. How long are you going to be out of commission?"

"Until the doctors say I'm well. I hope it's not going to be long. How are your cases going?"

"Just finished one up. Good money for a little work. I have another to hunt down a lost letter written by Abe Lincoln that went missing from a collector's home. Exciting stuff."

"I need something to do with my time, now."

"Can't you get your latest book finished? That's a good job for being in a wheelchair."

"I figured on that, since I can't go dancing for a while."

We heard the lobby door to our offices open, I couldn't turn my head enough to see who it was. Then I heard a friendly voice, it was Deacon.

"Jim, I heard from Lacey that you were disabled. Nice chair," he said coming up behind me. I wheeled the thing back and around to face him.

"Latest model. Buck said he was going to soup it up for me," I laughed.

"And I will," Buck said coming up the hallway to us with a pizza in hand.

"Buck, are you enjoying being a P.I. and investigating now?" Deacon asked.

41

"Loving it. I've got a case that the police don't want to bother with. A case of dognapping from a kennel."

"That's why I'm here. We had another kennel break-in last night. Unfortunately, an employee was murdered. This is no longer a matter of dognapping. Now it's homicide."

"How did you know we had this case?" I asked.

"Williams told me. He said he referred you." Deacon looked back to Buck and asked, "What do you have so far?"

"Honestly – nothing. I did find that my crime was planned well in advance." He told Deacon about the disabled camera.

"We got the same thing at our scene. Cameras were cut. The guy murdered must have interrupted them and he was hit on the head. Hard enough to kill him. I got CSI scouring the scene, but I think the perps covered themselves well. So, is Lynn in?"

"Don't know, none of us have been up front. She may be in her office," I said.

"Thanks, I'll go check. Buck, if you hear anything that can help, can you share?"

"No problem, I'll always help you."

"Thanks," he said and left us.

"Homicide. That's not good. But at least they didn't use a gun. Hitting the vic on the head sounds like a defensive move on their part. They just didn't realize how hard they hit him. Too bad for the vic."

"Whatever, shall we get out of here?" Buck said and went in to my office to get my crutches. I said good-bye to Earl and wheeled to the back door, Buck in tow. I yelled to Earl, "Let Lacey know I'm gone."

"I'll tell her after I finish my report," he replied with a laugh.

Buck hooked up the ramp and I wheeled into the van.

"You're going to have to use the van to get around, since you don't have your car," I said.

"No problem, I like being up here above the cars. I get to look down and see the legs of attractive women." He started the van and drove out, laughing.

*

Chapter 6

Buck managed to get me back into my home office. It wasn't too difficult moving me to my desk. The chair handled easily and it was the right height to get to my keyboard. Penny was standing in my doorway, still in her bathing suit. She loved to wear bathing suits. "I know what clothes I'm burying you in when you die," I said to her.

"I've got a red one-piece that I'll put away just for the occasion," she replied.

"Thanks, Buck." I said as he moved back to the door.

"My pleasure. Are you going to be all right tonight?" he asked.

"He'll probably sleep in the chair," Penny said.

"No, I'll manage to get in bed."

"If you kick me with that cast during the night, I'm pushing you out of bed," Penny said, sounding mockingly serious.

"I'll tie it down just for you, babe." I replied.

"Okay, I'll come by in the morning to help get you around," Buck said and then left.

"Buck is a good friend," Penny said. "You and he should run off together."

"He's not my type." I started up my computer. "What are you up to on your show tomorrow?"

"We're still covering the dog show. Gordy said he may have us do a remote from the show. I'll get to interview the dogs."

"Is a local dog show going to be entertaining enough for the nation to watch?" I asked.

"It's not just local. This is going to be big. The sponsor is moving this dog show around the country. They are going to Reno next. It's good for dog owners, and great publicity for the dog food company. There are the AKC sponsored shows, but this one gives all dogs a chance to shine. Anything on your dognapping ring yet?"

"Buck's got no leads, but he's going to go back at it tomorrow. There was another break-in at a kennel last night and an employee was murdered."

"How did you find this out?"

Kennel Murders

"Deacon stopped by to ask us about our case. This is getting serious."

"Murder is your curse," Penny said, trying to look serious.

"Stop that please, this had nothing to do with our case or my curse. Totally unrelated. It's Deacon's problem, not mine."

"You'll make it your problem, give it time." She picked up Willy, who was standing by her feet, and went out of the room.

"I will not," I yelled out to her. She didn't respond.

I was not comfortable in the bed. I usually turn a lot from one of my sides to the other. Moving the cast was annoying, so I slipped out of the bed and into my wheelchair. Penny mumbled something I couldn't hear, probably better that I didn't.

I wheeled out of the bedroom and into my office. I started up the computer and opened my latest story, may as well work if I couldn't sleep. I looked at the clock, it was just after three. Great, I was going to be up most of the night.

I wrote for a while, then finally felt tired. I wheeled out to the living room and over to the lounger that I had fallen asleep in many times. I slipped over on to the big chair and made myself comfortable by dropping the thing back. I guess I fell asleep shortly after. The next thing I knew, I was being awakened by Buck.

"Hey man, wake up. Can't sleep all day," he said.

"Yeah, and I can't sleep all night either. What time is it?"

"Just after seven. Penny left to go to the dog show. She said they're taping from there."

"Well, all for the better. Do you have anything to investigate on the kennel case?"

"Nope, I'm going to talk to Deacon, see if he has anything that may help. I've gotten no calls about any ransom, so maybe it's not that?" Buck helped me out of the lounger and over to my wheelchair.

"I really believe it's about ransom. But I've been known to be wrong. Just ask Penny."

Buck laughed as I wheeled to the kitchen. I was too low to work the toaster, so Buck made my toast for me. "If you want something to eat, help yourself." I said to him.

"I may whip up some eggs, if it's all right?"

I thought that sounded good. "Okay, make enough for me, too."

We ate our breakfast and then I got ready to go in to the office. Buck loaded me in the van and off we went.

~~*~~

Penny was trying to get around all the dogs in the back of the MGM Grand show arena. Willy was in his carrier and still having a fit over all the dogs he could see. Penny's camera crew was trying to keep up with her. Gordy even came out to participate in the show. The crew set up their equipment in the main arena while Gordy directed them.

"I got a live feed going back to the studio, so everything we do here will be taped back there. We can edit it before air time. Are you ready to shine?" Gordy said as he turned to Penny.

"I can't shine, I think I stepped in dog poop. I'll be a trooper and get over it. But you're going to buy me new shoes."

"Anything for my star. Now, I have the line-up of dogs coming out, so just read the names from the cards and smile." He handed Penny the cards and turned to his crew waiting for his command. Gordy thought it would be a good idea to have Penny introduce each dog before they went out to the floor to be judged and had it arranged with the show sponsors. Penny thought it was going to be a very long day. They looked to the master of ceremonies as the show started.

"Okay, we're rolling," Gordy said, and signaled the first contestant to come out as Penny looked into the camera.

"Hi people, I'm Penny Wickens, and this is my puppy, Willy. We're here at the Wilson Hearty Dog Chow sponsored All-breed dog show. This show isn't like the fancy dog shows you see from the American Kennel Club. Our competitors here are a combination of regular, everyday canines as well as some well-bred dogs, all competing for a few trophies and the chance to be featured on the packages of Wilson Hearty Dog Chow. Any dog can be entered and boy, there are a ton of dogs in this show." Penny smiled for the camera, trying to enjoy what she was doing.

The first woman came out with her dog. "Hi, and your name is?" She held the microphone to the woman.

"I'm Elaine Gajarsky and this is Bitsy, my Maltese."

"Thanks Elaine, take Bitsy out to the floor and wait." The woman did.

"Next?"

The woman came out and Penny asked the same question.

"I'm Michele Tater and this is Tobius, my golden Retriever and St. Bernard mix." Penny was trying to stay back from the huge dog. The woman moved out to the arena with her dog.

"Pat Pollington, from England and this is Bosun, an Enzo Black Lab," the next woman said.

"Thank you, Pat. And you are?" Penny asked the next contestant.

"Roberta Harder and my dog Titus Ambrosius, a Great Dane."

Again, Penny moved away from the huge dog.

Next out was a small dog so Penny relaxed. "Hi and you are?"

"Jessica Belous and this is Milton, my Shih Tzu."

"Thanks, head on out to the arena." Penny was already wearing down and Willy was struggling to get out of his purse. Penny wondered if she was going to survive this day.

*

Chapter 7

"Ladies and Gentlemen, dog lovers and fans. Welcome to the first annual Wilson Hearty Dog Chow All-breed Dog Show." Came a voice over the loudspeakers of the huge arena. "This is the first of many dog shows to be held around the country and we are honored to begin here in beautiful Las Vegas. If you'll turn your attention to the center ring, our master of ceremonies will start the show with a parade of our competitors."

Penny was watching from the side since she had finished welcoming the rest of the dogs and owners, who were out in the arena walking their dogs with pride. Gordy was on his phone talking to someone. He finished his call and went over to Penny.

Kennel Murders

"The live feed going back to the station went well and they are editing the tape now. You can rest until they ask you to present some of the awards and trophies," Gordy said.

Penny gave him an icy stare, "You never said anything about me handing out anything. I thought I was just going to intro the dogs and go home."

"Penny, dear, you are a celebrity and the sponsors want you to be part of the show. You are one of most nationally known TV personalities out of Vegas, and they need that to establish their credentials as a legit dog show. They are up against the AKC shows and the use of non-pedigreed dogs will touch dog owners everywhere. Besides, it's good for your show."

Penny sighed and said, "I'm taking Willy out for a dump. I'll think of you as he does it." She turned and went out of the arena to the door leading to the outside. The ticket takers knew her and waved her out.

Penny went to a grassy area on the side of the building and had to carefully walk around the dumpings from other dogs. It annoyed her that they hadn't picked up the little gifts, leaving the mess for someone else to clean up. Penny had plastic gloves in the dog carrier so she could clean up after Willy. She attached his leash and put him down, the small dog did his business. Penny picked up the small pile with the glove, then she wrapped it and put it in a pocket of the dog purse. She was thinking of possible ways to use the smelly package. Maybe to put it in Gordy's car? She'd love to watch Gordy's expression after getting a whiff of the doo-doo?

She put Willy back in the purse and went back to the show. The ticket takers let her pass and she found Gordy talking to some man in a suit.

"Penny!" Gordy call to her. She went closer. "Penny, this is Herbert Wilson, CEO of Wilson Hearty Dog Chow. He wanted to meet you."

"Hello, Mr. Wilson. Pleasure to meet you," Penny said as she took his hand to shake.

"Oh, please, call me Herb. I'm not that formal. I appreciate your being part of this show. I started it as a tribute to my dog, Bingo. He passed on and I thought about how he never knew the thrill of competing in a fancy dog show because he was just a mutt. Being in my position at a dog food company, I decided to do something about it. So here we are." He reached over to Willy and ruffled his head sticking out of the purse. "Cute dog," he said.

"Herb, that's very nice of you." Penny thought about all the goodwill and the profits these shows would bring for Herb. She smiled and said, "I'm sure mutt owners everywhere will thank you."

"Has Gordy told you about giving out the trophies?"

"Oh, yes he did, finally. I wasn't aware of it, but it sounds fine to me." Penny was glancing at Gordy, thinking more about the small pile of dog poop she carried and grinned.

"Well, I appreciate it. We're trying to establish ourselves in this new venture and your assistance is a big help. Dog lovers respect you for your love of your dog."

"Willy is like a son to me and my husband."

"And how the famous author and detective doing?" he asked.

"Right now, he's suffering from a broken leg. It happened during a battle with an evil-doer." Penny tried not to laugh.

"Wow, it must be exciting to be married to someone who leads an exciting life."

"You don't know the half of it," Penny said with a smirk.

"Well, I have to get back to the show. Please feel free to wander, I'll send someone to find you when it's time to give the trophies." He shook her hand again and went off.

Penny turned to Gordy. "I'll get you for this." She turned and went off, leaving Gordy alone.

Penny walked around checking out all the dogs and their owners. She decided it was true about how a dog and their owner started to look alike. She wondered if she was starting to look like Willy.

She was enjoying watching everything and being left alone as everyone was so busy with their animals that they ignored her. It felt nice to walk around without being stopped every few feet by an admiring fan. She came around a corner of the seating into a hallway and saw a few people standing around talking to a couple police officers. She recognized one of them as Ted, who had been involved in a couple of their cases. He was talking to three women.

She moved closer to listen. One woman was in tears and telling the officers something. Penny moved up behind Ted. He looked back, recognized Penny and smiled, then turned back to the woman.

"I'll file a report and we'll see what we can do to find him." Ted said as the woman handed him a picture. The woman went off with the two other women. Ted turned to Penny.

"Hey, Ms. Wickens, how are you doing?"

Kennel Murders

"I'm hanging in, Ted. What's going on?"

"Someone snatched her prize Shih Tzu. She turned away from the dog for a minute and when she looked back, he was gone. I can report it, but can't really put out a BOLO on a dog. I'll alert the MGM Grand security to be on watch. They may be able to pull the perp up on their cameras. How's Jim doing? We haven't had any good chases since Lynn left us."

"Jim has taken a back seat now that Lynn is working with us at the firm. Lynn is helping with the big cases and Jim is just moping around. He's on the disabled list right now, he broke his leg the other day."

"Ouch, I imagine that must be hard on him. Is Buck still with you guys?"

"He's Jim's nurse maid now," she laughed. "Although he's investigating a multiple dognapping from a kennel."

"Not the one where there was a murder?"

"No, a different one. Well, you should go start the wheels of justice for the missing dog."

"Right. It was good to see you again." He went off with the other officer and Penny turned her gaze to watch the woman who lost her dog.

She tried to imagine what it would be like to have Willy stolen. She knew she wouldn't like it and would do what she could to get him back. She patted her Smith and Wesson .38 in her jacket pocket and smiled.

*

Chapter 8

Buck was sitting with Deacon in Lynn's old office. "So, have they found a place for you yet?" Buck asked.

"You're looking at it. Captain Weber decided to keep me here to fill Lynn's shoes, so I stay in homicide. I didn't want to go to Vice or OCU, they both had captains I wasn't fond of. I can tolerate Weber, I'm used to him and he's used to me."

"Do you think Warren, Williams and the rest of the men are going to have a problem with you as their Lieutenant? Is it going to be a problem being their superior officer over them?"

"They've all given me their blessings. Besides, they know if they gave me any problems,

Lynn would come in and bust their chops," Deacon said with a laugh. "Since she's not a cop now, she doesn't care. Anything new on your dognapping case?"

"Nope. I was hoping you'd have something to tell me."

"We did some digging around and found that there has been a puppy mill ring going on somewhere in the Vegas vicinity. Unfortunately, every time they've gone in to bust the perps, they vanish and move locations. Someone is feeding them info from within the police ranks. That's my opinion."

"Have you notified the pet shops around Vegas?" Buck asked.

"I sent some of the guys out to sweep the stores to see if anyone has tried to sell any dogs recently. Either they haven't or the shop owners are lying. I told the men to give stern warnings about accepting any stolen dogs. We'll prosecute anyone doing so."

Greg Warren stuck his head in the door and said, "Hey Deacon, got a call from one of those pet shops about a man coming in with a dog to sell. The owner said it was an expensive breed. The man told the owner that he couldn't take care of the dog anymore."

"Thanks Greg, give me the address, I'll go talk to the owner." Deacon turned to Buck, "Feel like taking a ride?"

"If it will help, sure." He stood as Deacon went to get the address. They went out to get a car from the motor pool. Deacon took out the Dodge Interceptor, he liked that car. Buck didn't object.

They drove down to Henderson and into a shopping plaza where the Friendly Pets Store was located. It looked clean and professional on the outside. They entered and found a salesperson tending to some customers checking out a couple dogs. Deacon held his badge up and the man came to them after excusing himself.

"Are you the owner?" Deacon asked.

"I am. Fred Brenner." He held out his hand to shake.

"I'm Lieutenant DeAngelo, and this is Mr. Carson. You called about a possible stolen dog?"

"Yes, please follow me." He led them to a back room where there were a variety of dogs in cages. He went to one cage on the floor and pointed. "This is the dog I had a feeling about. The police officers who were in yesterday told me to be on the lookout for pure-bred dogs."

"What is it?" Deacon asked, kneeling down to look at the dog.

"A Shar Pei. It's definitely a show dog. Not at all like the type of dog the man who brought him in would seem to have. He appeared to be sleazy to me."

"Looks like a mound of wrinkled flesh," Buck said with a smile.

"That's their distinctive feature," the store owner said.

Deacon took out a note pad and checked it against his list of dogs stolen from the kennel where the murder took place. "It's not on my list. Buck do you have a list?"

"I sure do." He took out a piece of paper and looked it over. "Spell that for me please?" Buck asked the owner. He did and Buck said, "Yep, it's on my list. I'll call the kennel owner and have her come over to check the dog."

Deacon stood up and said, "Did you buy the dog from the man?"

"I gave him a B.S. story about having to keep the dog in quarantine to be sure he didn't have Canine Parvovirus disease. He gave me a blank stare and I said I'd keep the dog overnight and he could come back tomorrow morning and I'd pay him, if the dog doesn't die. He put up a small argument, but he finally gave in."

"Great, we'll be back here tomorrow then." Deacon said. "I'll place a couple detectives in the pet shop disguised as helpers for you. Will that be alright?"

"No problem. I'm not fond of these puppy mills, they make it tough for us legitimate pet shops to offer healthy pets to our customers. They're cruel and mistreat the poor dogs they get. I wish there was some way to shut all those jerks down. I'll expect your men by eight, when I open. I figure he'll be at the door waiting."

"I'll be sure to have them here early. Thanks for your help. We'll also have the kennel owner here to identify the dog. Do you have an ID chip reader?"

"I do, and already scanned the dog." He turned and got a piece of paper from a counter and handed it to Deacon. "Here's the info from the scan. It should help your kennel owner to identify the dog."

"This will help us greatly." Deacon said.

"I heard a kennel employee was murdered during a break-in. Do you think this person could be in on that situation?"

Kennel Murders

"We'll find out tomorrow. Okay, we'll leave you to your customers. Thanks again." Deacon and Buck left the store and walked back to the car.

They sat there for a moment, then Buck said, "These crooks didn't take very many dogs to make much money from them. Have you had reports from private dog owners about their dogs going missing?"

"Generally, they don't report it to the police. They end up posting pictures around or putting ads in the classifieds. We really don't have any figures on how many dogs go missing from their homes. I see what you're getting at though. This may not even be a puppy mill. Maybe they're grabbing the dogs for quick cash."

"They'd get the high end expensive dogs from a kennel, I just don't figure they'd make a lot of money off them." Buck said.

"Well, the theft of the dogs is not my case, I'm hunting a murder suspect. You have the doggy case." Deacon grinned and started the car.

They drove back to the precinct with very little conversation, both men lost in thought. Buck was hoping the suspect who was going to go to the pet store would have some answers.

"I'm going to my car to call the kennel lady and have her go see if the dog at the pet store is one of her missing dogs." Buck said as they stood by the car.

"Let me know, so I'll have the info whether this involves your kennel or mine."

"I'm sure the thieves were at both kennels. I don't see two separate puppy mills breaking into kennels on the same night." Buck paused then said, "Hey Deacon, I got to tell you something."

"Is it about you and Maria?"

Buck was surprised by his question. "Did you talk to her?"

"No, I could just tell you two were drifting apart. Maria is wound pretty tight and loves her job more than anything. I saw you two apart a lot so I figured you were splitting."

"You okay with it?" Buck asked.

"I'd like to see my little sister settle down, but she's always been a wild child. I good with it. It seems like I know you better than her. I see more of you, so I'm good. Where you going to stay?"

"I've got a line on an apartment up on Sahara that one of my guards lives in. So I'm getting ready to take it and move."

"Well, if you need help, let me know."

"I will, buddy. Thanks."

Buck said his good-byes and went to his car.

*

Chapter 9

Buck sat in his car and pulled out his cell phone. He dialed the phone number from the sheet of paper he had with the list of missing dogs. As the line rang he looked at the slip of paper with the information from the ID scan. It made no sense to him, he hoped the kennel woman would be able to figure it out.

"Happy Puppy Dog Kennel, may I help you?" came a pleasant woman's voice.

"Ms. Valstad, please."

"You got her," she replied.

"Ma'am, I'm George Carson, from Richards Investigations. Do you have a minute to talk?"

"I do, what have you found?"

"Well, I think we found one dog. I have a scan code from the dog's ID chip. Can you tell me if it's one of the missing dogs."

"Sure, what's the code?"

Buck read from the slip as the woman listened, then she said, "Was it a Shar Pei?"

"That's right." Buck replied.

She was silent for a moment, Buck figured she was still checking. "Yes, it was one of the dogs. This is great. Where is the animal now?"

"It's part of a murder investigation for now, but I can assure you the dog is safe and sound with people who know how to take care of dogs. I'll have to call you back tomorrow about picking up the animal."

The woman thanked Buck and they disconnected. Buck hoped the dog wouldn't be held as evidence in the police case. He dialed Deacon to give him the news, hoping it would help. Deacon was glad that the dog was part of the crime, now he had something to pin on the perp in the morning. They made arrangements to meet at the pet shop and finished the call. Buck was happy there was a crack in the case.

~~*~~

Penny was walking around the arena field watching the dogs strut and jump through the routines their owners trained them to do. She laughed at the sight of a couple men with scoops and bags following the parade of dogs around, waiting to pick up the little gifts left behind. She thought about Willy's little gift and considered handing it to one of the pooper scoopers. Then she thought maybe she'd keep it for a better use.

"Penny!" Came a voice behind her. She turned to see it was Lynn.

"Lynn, what are you doing here?"

"Lacey told me you were going to be here, so I came to watch the dogs and protect you," she said with a grin.

"Didn't you have a case to solve?"

"I finished it up. I was giving the report to Lacey and asked if she knew where you were. She told me about this."

"I was ready to leave earlier, but unfortunately, I have to stay until the end and hand out trophies."

"How did you get roped into that?"

"Gordy, of course. He neglected to mention it to me until after I got here. Did you hear about Jim?"

"I saw him at the office. He wasn't happy to be out of commission, but he was having a good time riding the wheelchair around. I expect him to be pulling wheelies in the parking lot."

"Boys and their toys. How's Deacon doing?"

"Good, he's taking my old job in homicide and happy about it. I hope Weber doesn't drive him crazy. Deacon can be a little nervous at times."

They turned to the side when they heard a woman yelling something. Penny and Lynn went over to the woman standing on the other side of the short barrier that kept people off the competing field.

"My dog! Someone took my dog! Please, call the police!" she was saying.

Lynn's cop instinct took over and she went around the barrier to the woman, with Penny following.

"Ma'am, calm down and talk to me," Lynn said calmly.

"Are you a cop?"

"I was. I'm a private investigator now. Never mind that, what happened?"

"I set my Shih Tzu on that chair and went to get her brush, I just turned away for a few seconds, and she was gone. Can you help?"

Lynn pulled her phone and hit speed dial for her old precinct. She got dispatch and explained the situation. She hung up and said, "There should be a couple officers here shortly. Give them the description and what happened. I'll wait with you."

Lynn turned to Penny. "I didn't think there would be any excitement at a dog show."

"You should have been here earlier. Another dog was taken. Could this be a crime wave? Jim told me about the kennel thefts."

"Yeah, he told me Buck was on that case. He said he thinks it's for ransom of the dogs. What better place to get expensive dogs than a dog show? I'll make some calls and see if they can get a few officers to patrol the area."

"Maybe I can get the sponsor to make an announcement to watch for the thieves," Penny said, tightening her hold on Willy.

"It would help. Go take care of that and I'll wait here for the officers."

Penny went off and found the show officials and explained the situation. They went to the master of ceremonies and told him what to say. The M.C. took the microphone and made the hasty announcement, warning people to be alert for anyone looking suspicious and to keep an eye on their dogs.

Penny was heading back to Lynn when she ran into Herb Wilson.

"I can't believe something like this would mar my show. Damn criminals. I'll call and have some security firm come in to keep an eye on the contestants."

Penny reached in her purse and took out a card with the firm's number, handing it to him. "Herb, my husband's investigating company also has a guard service. I'm sure they could have men here fast. I'll call the man in charge and see what he can do."

"That's great. Have them find me and I'll get them set up. We still have tomorrow to run the show, so they will be needed. Whatever the cost, I can't have this giving a bad name to my shows."

Kennel Murders

"I'll get right on it." Penny said as Wilson went off. She took out her cell phone and called Buck.

About forty minutes later, Buck arrived with twelve uniformed security men that he was able to get together at the last minute. Penny introduced him to Wilson and the two men went off to discuss the arrangements.

Penny turned to see Lynn coming over to her. "Did the officers help the woman with her missing dog?" Penny asked.

"Not much they could do." Lynn said. "They're going to check with hotel security to see if they have anything showing on their cameras. I'm sure it won't help. Since the dog is valued at a couple grand, that makes it a felony. So there'll be more investigating by Robbery Division. I see Buck and his men are here. I talked to the head of hotel security and they are going to add a few of their men to the festivities."

"This is not what I expected this morning when I got here. Gordy owes me big time."

Lynn laughed and said, "I can see Jim riding his wheelchair around the place trying to track down criminals."

"Looks like we're the detectives now. Shall we investigate?"

*

Chapter 10

Buck had his guards distributed around the area after explaining to them what they were watching for. Hotel security had been advised of the situation and intermingled with the contestants where they gathered before they went out to show their dogs. All the exits were covered and the guards had radios in case of another attack. Hopefully, they'd be able to communicate with each other and stop anyone from leaving with a stolen dog.

"They've got the place covered now," Lynn said to Penny as they stood by the arena. "I don't think anyone will try another snatch with all the guards around."

"Wilson will have to hire guards for all his shows now, to prove he's serious about protecting the contestants." Penny said.

Kennel Murders

Buck went up to the women and gave them his walrus grin.

"What are you so happy about?" Penny asked.

"We may have a break in the dognapping case and maybe the murder. One of the hoods tried to sell a dog to a local pet shop. The owner called the cops and the perp is due to come back in the morning to pick up the money for the dog. The only thing he's going to pick up is handcuffs. If we can make him talk, we may find the other dogs and a murderer."

"That's good. Hopefully it's the same people who took the dogs here. Maybe we can get some owners back to their animals." Lynn said.

Buck reached over and ruffled Willy's head in his pouch. "Keep an eye on this one. I'd hate to see anything happen to him." He looked over to one of the entrances and saw Trapper and Earl coming in. He yelled to them, startling people around him. They heard Buck bellow and came over.

"Well, if Jim were here we'd have the whole firm," Lynn said. "This is the most I've seen of our group together since Jim's anniversary party last month."

Trapper spoke first. "We were in the office turning in our reports to Lacey and Jim came rolling out to tell us all about his accident. Then Lacey said Penny was at this affair, so we thought we'd get away from the office and come over to admire the dogs."

"You left my poor husband all alone?" Penny asked.

"Lacey is with him," Earl said.

"As I said, alone. Lacey would rather he weren't around," Penny said and turned to Buck. "Are you doing anything important right now?" He said no. "Why don't you go get Jim in the van and bring him over here? He may get a kick out of being among people."

"You got it, boss's wife," he said with another grin. "I'll be back." He left.

"Anything we can do to help?" Trapper asked.

"Just watch out for dog snatchers. Two have been taken so far." Lynn said.

"Two? With all these people around, they're either brave or stupid. Anything off the security cameras?" Earl asked.

"The officers who took the report checked with security and they got a shot of the first perp, but he had his head covered by a hoodie. No word or photos on the second snatch. Why don't you two do something to help by looking around? Maybe you'll catch the next perp."

"Think it will happen again?" Penny asked.

"These people hit two kennels last night, murdering an employee in one, then there were grab and runs here on two dogs so far. This is accelerating into an all-out crime wave. Is there a big market for dogs?" Lynn asked Penny.

"When you consider how much these dogs are worth over their life-time, it's worth it." Penny said. "I had a dog breeder on one of my shows and she explained how much a breeder could make for an AKC registered dog."

"But this show isn't an American Kennel Club sanctioned show." Lynn said.

"Sure, but most of these dogs are registered. The owners would love to have their dog pictured on a bag of dog chow. It's a matter of pride for them. So, they bring in their AKC registered animal and enter in the competition. It's not much trouble for a criminal to find out which dogs are show dogs." Penny said.

"Okay, what would these perps do with the dogs?" Earl asked.

"Breed them, sell them, try for ransom from the owners. Who knows? We won't know until something happens. Buck said they had a suspect, but they can't get to him until the morning. It may pay off." Penny said.

Lynn was watching the crowd and saw someone she never grew tired of seeing, Deacon. "Earl, would you go get my husband, he looks lost," she said, pointing. Earl laughed and went to get the big man.

They came back and Deacon gave Lynn a hug. "Hey, you're a cop on duty, you can't be fraternizing." Lynn said. "What are you doing here?"

"Part of my murder investigation. There are dogs here and I'm hunting a group of murdering dognappers. What are you doing here?" Deacon said, stepping back from his wife.

"I came to give Penny protection for her being a celebrity in this show. Earl and Trapper are just slumming. Right guys?"

The two men nodded in approval. Deacon laughed. "Why isn't Jim here? He has a wheelchair doesn't he?"

"Buck went to get him, just to get him out of the office." Penny said. "He should be here in a while."

"So, the whole team is going to take this case on. I hope it gets settled soon, then. It will save me the trouble." Deacon said with a smile.

"Save you from having to work," Lynn said.

"That, too. Now, fill me in on what is going on here."

Lynn and Penny took turns explaining the day's events and Deacon just stood listening.

"This is turning into a major crime wave. Besides the theft of the dogs, we have a murder. Our suspect, who we will nab tomorrow morning, will hopefully give us some answers." Deacon said.

"Unfortunately, that doesn't help the poor people who had their furry children stolen." Penny said. "I never had children, but I know how I would feel if Willy was taken. He's as close to me as a child would be."

"Just keep an eye on him. We won't let anything happen to him, too." Lynn said.

~~*~~

Buck wheeled me into the van and fastened my wheelchair down so I wouldn't fly around when he whipped through the streets.

"So what's going on?" I asked.

"Dogs are going missing, stolen while the owners turned away for a second," Buck said.

"Sounds planned. The perps had to know what dogs to grab. Who would have access to that information?"

"Don't know, we can find out when we get there."

"Who all is there?"

Trapper, Earl, Lynn and Penny."

"So that's why the office is deserted. I thought it was just me chasing everyone out."

"Nope, only Lacey would want to leave because you are in the office." Buck smiled.

"Does Lacey despise me that much?" I asked.

"Hell, no. She thinks of you as a father figure. Most young women don't like their fathers hanging around them. She and I have talked and she cares about you as much as the father she never had. You are important to her. She can just be a little sarcastic at times. You aren't a friend, you're her daddy."

I thought about that. I guess I'd have to try being a little friendlier to her.

*

Chapter 11

I was getting a little carried away with my wheelchair, zooming through the parking garage and around the sidewalk of the MGM Grand as Buck was trying to keep up. I had a blast driving down the parking ramps while Buck was yelling at me to be careful. "I already have a broken leg, what worse could happen?"

"How about a broken neck," Buck said in response to my logic. "I'm not going to wipe your butt if you can't do it yourself." He went to the entrance and held the door open for me.

I rolled into the building and was greeted by Penny and Lynn. "How'd you know I was here?"

"Buck called me while you were bombing around the parking structure," Penny replied.

"It was the first area big enough to put this baby through its paces."

Penny took Willy from his purse and handed him to me. She slung the dog purse on the chair and said, "You're now responsible for our child. Guard him with your life. Which won't be worth much if someone grabs him." She gave me a big grin and then filled me in on what had transpired before I got there.

"Where are Trapper and Earl now?" I asked.

"Somewhere around the building chasing dognappers." Lynn said. "Deacon was here, but he went to talk to hotel security about surveillance cameras."

"You know Lacey's going to ask who's paying us for this case." I said.

"Buck can add it to his bill for guard services. There are enough employees from Jim Richards Investigations and Security running around here today. This is a big deal and this job will take all of us." Penny said with a grin.

"You can investigate," I said. "I'm going to ride around and look at all the dogs. Remember, I'm still on vacation this week. So, no work for me." I said.

"You didn't get much work done around the house either."

I stuck my tongue out at her and rode off with Willy on my lap. She stood laughing. Buck followed me, probably to be sure I didn't hurt myself again.

~~*~~

Lynn asked Penny, "Shall we go check out the contestants and their dogs? See which are valuable enough to steal."

"Lead on, Sherlock."

"Follow me, Watson." Lynn said and they went to the waiting area where the dogs were warming up to perform.

All of Buck's guards knew Penny and Lynn, so they would smile and occasionally wave. The two went to a woman sitting on a chair with her dog next to her. The woman was grooming the dog and looked up to them.

"You better not be thinking of taking my dog," the woman said. Then she saw Penny. "Oh my God, you're Penny Wickens."

"Yes I am, and you are?"

"Taisha Cullum and this is Majesty, my poodle-terrier mix. Do you know what's going on with the dogs disappearing?"

"All we know is there may be people taking dogs for profit. Mostly the AKC registered dogs." Penny replied.

"Well, my dog isn't a pure-bred, so I guess I don't have to worry."

"I'm sure your dog will be safe. Excuse us, we need to walk around."

They left the woman and went to a man standing next to a Labrador Retriever. He looked to Penny and smiled. "Are you investigating the theft of the dogs now?"

"Pardon me?" Penny said.

"I know you are married to Jim Richards and act as part of his team of investigators when you're not on camera."

"You seem to know me, you are?"

Kennel Murders

"Ray Zink, I'm a fan of yours and I read your husband's books. I also read the newspapers every time they mention him saving Las Vegas."

"Yes, he loves to fight off terrorists and assassins. Beautiful dog you have."

"Yes, her name is Sandy. My baby. I'm not in the show, I just wanted to come down to watch. Anything on the thefts yet?"

"Still investigating. Real life isn't like TV. Crimes don't get solved in an hour. Or so my husband keeps saying."

"I did see a strange man leaving through one of the exits with a dog under his arm. He didn't look much like a dog owner by the way he was carrying it."

Lynn spoke now. "Did you get a look at his face?"

"Enough to identify him. I can give a description if needed," he said.

"Great, it will add to the case. Hold on." She pulled her cell phone out and called Deacon. She explained what she had and said she'd wait for him. "I called my husband, he's the lead detective in a murder investigation. The murder took place at a dog kennel and may have something to do with the rash of thefts here. He's on his way."

"Anything I can do to help," he said.

They talked about the dog show until Deacon came. Lynn introduced Ray to Deacon.

"I don't want to take you away from the show, but I have a sketch artist coming in. Hope you can help."

Deacon took the man to a place that they could talk and left Penny and Lynn alone.

"See, we investigated and found a lead," Penny said with a grin.

"Maybe we should start our own investigating firm."

"I don't think Jim would be able to handle the competition, we'd put him out of business," Penny said, laughing. Her smile turned to a frown as an announcement went out over the P.A. asking for Penny Wickens to go to the judge's booth.

"I hope they don't want me to judge. I had enough of that with the Elvis contest and the talent show. Shall we go see what they want?"

"Lead the way," Lynn said and they went off.

Kennel Murders

~~*~~

I was finding it a bit difficult to maneuver through the crowd in the chair. People just didn't look where they were going, and never looked down to see me. Buck finally moved to my side from the back.

"I'll start whacking anyone who runs into you," he said with a grunt. I was concerned for those people who did. But the sight of the huge man next to me opened the crowd like Moses parting Red Sea. We rolled—well, I rolled, and Buck just kind of moseyed —around looking at all the dogs being primped and groomed to strut the dog walk.

"So, what would these criminals do with the dogs once they have them?" Buck asked.

"I think they'd want to sell them or ransom them. They couldn't really breed them. It takes time to raise a dog and then to make that dog an AKC registered dog. They'd also have to forge pedigree papers to show the dog's bloodline. But most people that buy a 'registered' dog never really check the origin of the papers. Most families like to tell their friends they have a fancy dog of good breeding when the dog actually came from a puppy mill."

"That's just stupid. It encourages crooks to steal dogs."

"Yes, it is, but people don't think about consequences like that. Just like people who run into me. I feel sorry for people who are permanently disabled and have to do this every day." I saw Deacon walking out of the arena with a man. I motioned to Buck and we headed their way.

Out in the hallway, I saw Deacon talking to the man. I wheeled over to them.

"Hey, Jim, see you got out finally. This man saw one of the dognappers and can identify him."

"Mr. Richards, I'm Ray Zink and I'm a fan of your books. Did a criminal take out your leg?" the man said.

I really hated to spoil his image of me and said "It was in the line of duty." I heard Buck snicker behind me.

*

Chapter 12

I turned my head towards Buck, he shut up. I looked back to the man. "Mr. Zink, it's a pleasure to know you're helping the police find a possible killer and dognappers."

"It's my pleasure. I'm a dog lover and this is not something I approve of. Glad to help."

Deacon asked the man to follow him. He said to Buck and me, "Got the sketch artist going to the security office, so see you two later." They went off.

"Shall we go watch the dogs?" Buck asked.

"Lead the way, big guy."

We went into the auditorium and over to the barrier. Luckily it was short enough for me to see over. I could see Penny standing out in the middle of the arena with two men. One was holding a microphone. I set Willy up on the barrier so he could see his mother.

"Ladies and Gentlemen, we have the results for today's judging. We are fortunate to have as a guest presenter, Las Vegas' favorite talk show host, Penny Wickens."

The crowd shouted approval and clapped. Penny waved to the throng of people and took the microphone when the man handed it out to her.

"Thank you, Lyle. I'm honored to be here and to award the trophies to the dogs that the judges deemed worthy of first and second places. Shall we start?" She looked to Herb Wilson standing next to her. He smiled and signaled to his people standing with the contestants. They led the owners and their dogs out to the center of the arena and lined them up.

Penny waited until they were all out and then read from cards she had. "Our first award goes to the miniature dog category, too bad my Toy Yorkie, Willy, isn't here."

Buck yelled loudly, "He's over here." The crowd laughed and Penny waved to Willy and me. Willy did a little dance on the barrier.

"Okay, the first place award goes to Michael Vannoy and his mini-poodle, Valentino." The crowd applauded and Vannoy moved out of the line and took his trophy.

He went off, being led by two attractive women. Then Penny announced, "The second place award goes to Lizz Dempsey and her Chihuahua,

Kennel Murders

Fred." The young girl came forward and got her trophy. She went off with the same women.

Penny announced the mid-sized dog category. First place went to Karen Meinberg-Richwine and her dog Tobey, a Cairn Terrier. Then, second place to Clare Moody with Belle, a Border Collie. They accepted their trophies.

The large dog category went to Kathy Moore and her Boxer, Ali for first. Second went to Jan Kimball for her Doberman, Kitty.

"Now that's a good name for a Doberman... Kitty. I hope that dog is in therapy." The crowd laughed as the owners went to get their trophies. "That's all for the first day of competition, folks. Hope you can come back tomorrow for more. The dogs that will be featured on Wilson Hearty Dog Chow packaging will be determined then, along with more awards for our furry friends. The sponsor, Herb Wilson, asked me to thank you all for coming. All dogs that competed today will be awarded certificates for appearing in the competition. Thank you and drive safely."

Penny handed the microphone back to the M.C., Lyle. He smiled and went off. Penny came over to Buck, Willy, and me and grabbed on to Willy.

"Where's Lynn? I asked Penny.

"Standing behind you," came a voice from behind me. I craned my neck to see Lynn standing behind Buck. She came up to the barrier next to us.

"How long have you been back there?" I asked.

"Long enough. Did you find Deacon?" she said.

"We did. He went off to security with someone who can identify one of the dognappers."

"Really, a break in the case?" Lynn said.

"Is this really a case?" Penny asked.

"Despite the fact that we weren't hired to investigate this dog and pony show, I think we are doing a service to the animal community," I said.

"Where were there ponies?" Buck asked.

"It's an expression, Buck." I turned to Lynn. "Can you go see what's happening with Deacon and the witness?"

Lynn looked at Penny. "Care to join me?"

Penny picked up Willy and said, "Let's go, Sherlock."

Kennel Murders

"On our way, Watson."

The women left Buck and me alone. I wheeled around and faced Buck. "What shall we do now?"

"Want to go to a strip club? You'd probably get a lot of sympathy there."

"But then I'd get no sympathy at home, so that's out. I could use something to eat. Shall we go get some food?"

"Works for me. Just go slow on the parking ramps."

"I think we need to wait a while. With all these people leaving at the same time, we'd be held up for an hour. Let's go explore the MGM hotel." I said, and steered the wheelchair toward to the exit to the hotel. People were struggling to get out. I hated crowds, so we held back until it was clear.

Once I saw an opening in the crowd, I jetted out the doors yelling for people to move. They jumped away from me. I didn't care if I startled them, they were rude to me earlier. Buck was keeping up and was probably ready to whack anyone in my way.

We went around the lobby of the MGM Grand and through the exhibit of the lions. The whole lobby had a jungle theme to it. I loved going through there. We were just ready to head out when I saw someone I thought about talking to. Cindy Valstad, owner of the Happy Puppy Kennel.

She saw Buck and me, waved, and came over to us. She had a dog on a leash, looking like a ball of fur from the front.

"Mr. Carson, Mr. Richards, are you here investigating?" she asked.

"I'm watching dogs, Mr. Carson is investigating," I said with a grin.

"Please call me Buck, everybody does. What kind of dog is that?"

"Muttley is his name, he's a Shih Tzu. Am I supposed to do something about the dog you found?"

"The Shar Pei? The police are investigating and you should have it back soon. You'll probably have to identify the dog so they can arrest the person trying to sell the dog. I'll call you when I find out what's going to happen." Buck said.

"Thank you. Do you think this will lead to the other dogs?"

"I certainly hope so," Buck said with a grin.

"You two will have to excuse me, I need to go find my wife," I said.

Buck looked to Valstad and said. "I'm his nurse, so I need to go with him. I'll call you as soon as the police let me know what's going on. Don't Worry, I'll find the dogs for you."

She thanked us and went off. "Do you think you will be able to find the missing dogs," I said as I drove the wheelchair towards the security offices.

"I'll find out in the morning after we nab the doggy seller. Deacon will get him to talk, I'm sure." Buck said as he followed me.

"You put a lot of faith in Deacon," I said.

"If he doesn't get some answers from the perp, maybe Deacon will let me beat the crap out of him," Buck gave me his best walrus smile as he opened the door to the security offices.

*

Chapter 13

I rolled into the office and found a woman at a desk giving me a suspicious eye. Then she saw Buck behind me and took on a whole different look, shock.

"I'm Jim Richards, from Richards' Investigations and this man is my associate, George Carson. I'm looking for Detective DeAngelo, who's here with a police sketch artist." I said, smiling.

She then smiled back and said, "Yes, they're in the conference room with our Captain. Go down the hallway. It's the third door on the right."

I thanked her and wheeled down the hallway. As I got to the opened door, I could see Penny and Lynn standing just inside the opening. Penny looked over and gave me a grin. She was holding Willy and came out to meet us.

"How the sketch artist doing?" I asked.

"They're working on it. The man, Mr. Zink, must have gotten a good look at the suspect. He's really describing the perp."

Lynn came out. "Hotel security just lets you just roll around in that thing?" she asked with a grin.

"No one has stopped me so far. I'm getting tired, this chair is getting to me. I think I'll have Buck take me home and you two can do the investigating. I'll be back home working on my next book."

Penny said, "Good, you need the money."

"For what? The money you'll get when I die?"

"Of course. Now scoot, or roll, or whatever you do in that thing," Penny said.

I looked up to Buck. "I know when I'm not wanted. Take me home, Jeeves."

"Jeeves? What, I'm your butler now?" Buck said with a laugh. He came up behind me and grabbed the handles and turned me around.

"I can do that," I said as I grabbed the control and moved the chair forward. "Don't stay out too late," I yelled back to Penny as I maneuvered down the hall to the exit and out.

~~*~~

Deacon was grinning widely as the sketch artist worked on the composite image on his laptop. He looked back at Penny and Lynn who had re-entered the room.

"Amazing programs they have for computers. Nowadays, the sketch artist doesn't have to draw with a pencil and pad. The computer does the work for you. Once he's finished, he'll do a printout or send the image to the precinct and it will be on every LEIN computer in patrol cars all over the valley."

"They'll do a facial recognition?" Lynn asked.

"Of course, we need to know who we're dealing with. I'm betting he's a small time hood, but he could be part of a gang. Two kennels hit and the dogs taken today. There's something happening." Deacon said. "I'm not figuring how this crime can be a money maker?"

"Lots of money in fancy breeds of dogs." Penny said. "Not that I would think that a gang would spend time stealing dogs to make money, but it's a strange world."

"Well, in the morning we should have one of the perps in custody," Deacon said as the sketch artist called to him. Deacon went to the computer and looked at the finished product. "Weasel looking, isn't he?"

Kennel Murders

Ray Zink said, "It's very close to what I saw. Amazing machines, these computers."

"Yes, they are and thank you for your help." Deacon led the man to the door going out and bid him farewell. He came back to the room and told the tech to send the image off. He turned to the women and said, "Interested in something to eat?"

~~*~~

I was wearing down and it was getting late. I wondered where Penny was and then I heard the driveway alarm go off. I rolled into the kitchen and reset the alarm as Penny came into the room from the garage.

"Anything on the thefts?" I asked.

"Deacon is going to have the photo examined and hopefully they will have an I.D. to catch the perp."

"I love it when you talk cop," I said.

She leaned down and kissed my bald head. "I'm going to bed. I had to endure all those dogs today. I don't even want to see Willy." She put the dog down on my lap and went off to the bedroom.

I looked down to our pet and smiled. "She loves you, but I think you need to stay away tonight."

He looked up to me and yipped. I reached down and patted his head, then rolled into the other room.

~~*~~

Buck was feeling good. It was a sunny Saturday morning and he was going to help catch a dog thief. He was driving his classic T-Bird out to the pet shop in Henderson to meet with Deacon. He pulled into the shopping plaza and saw Deacon standing with a couple of his detectives. He looked across the street and could see the patrol car, probably waiting for orders to move in and transport the prisoner to the precinct.

Buck got out of his car and ambled towards the detectives. "Good morning, gents," he said with a big grin.

"Hey, Buck. Ready to watch justice spin its wheels?" Deacon said.

"I don't think you meant it that way," Buck laughed.

Deacon thought about what he said. "Yeah, I didn't. Well, the shop owner hasn't shown up yet, so we wait."

"I thought he said he'd be here before eight? It's now after eight."

"Yeah, he may have been delayed." He turned to one of his men and said. "Williams, go take a look in the back and see if he went in that way."

Williams went off around the building. Since the pet shop was on the end of the plaza building the walk didn't take too long.

"Any word on the sketch?" Buck asked.

"Nothing for face recognition yet. They're working on it, but if he's not in the system, they may not find him."

"But if he's a criminal, he must have a mug shot on file."

"One would think so. But he may have eluded the police in the past. I'm hoping he has a record." Deacon said and turned his attention to the store when he heard Williams unlocking the store entrance door. "What the hell?"

They went to the front door as the detective said, "I found the back door open. You need to get in here."

Everyone filed into the building as Williams led them to a back room. They found the pet shop owner on the floor. "I already called for a bus, he's alive, barely. Looks like he was hit from behind."

Deacon looked over to the cage that held the Shar Pei the day before. "Crap, the dog is gone. The perp must have been waiting for the owner, hit him when he came in. Williams, go check the register and see if there's any money in it." He turned to Buck. "He may have not put money in the register yet, but I'm betting on theft."

One of the other detectives came out of a small office. "Deacon, the safe in here is open and empty."

Deacon went into the office and looked into the floor safe. It had papers but no money. "I'm wondering if this was a set-up to rob the owner. Bring in a dog to sell and then grab money if the owner bought the animal."

He went back out to the man on the floor. He knelt down and moved the man gently to see if he was awake yet. He gave no indication of waking. Deacon looked up to Buck and said, "Looks like we'll have to wait."

Chapter 14

The Med-techs had the pet shop owner on a gurney and placed him in the EMS unit. One man said he may be in a coma, too soon to tell. Deacon had called for the CSI unit and they went to work investigating the scene.

"Well, this doesn't help us. I hope they get a hit off the sketch, at least," Deacon said, looking perturbed. He and Buck left the building and stood out front.

"I've got my men back at the MGM arena for today's dog show. Maybe they'll catch a dognapper." Buck said, looking hopeful.

"It would help, I've got nothing until the facts come in. I feel like going to the kennel where you were hired to investigate. I only saw my crime scene."

"I can lead you there," Buck said.

Deacon told Williams to take the lead and then he and Buck went to the cars. They drove over to the Happy Puppy Kennel and parked out front. Deacon followed Buck into the building.

There was a young girl at the front desk. "Is Ms. Valstad in?" Buck asked.

The girl gave a programed smile and said, "No, she's off today. Can I help you?"

Deacon moved forward and showed his badge. "We're here to look over the scene of the crime from the other day. We need to go into your kennel."

"Oh, yes, sure, I guess it's all right," the girl stammered.

She took us to the area where they kept the dogs in cages. Deacon thanked the girl and told her, "We can go from here."

The girl left them and went back to the front. The men walked around the cages, checking each one.

"What exactly are you looking for?" Buck asked Deacon.

"I haven't the faintest idea. But visiting this scene may help to stimulate my thoughts."

"We could go to a strip club. That would stimulate your thoughts," Buck said with a laugh.

Kennel Murders

"Sure, and Lynn would stimulate my ass." Deacon said. "She's not as forgiving as Penny when you and Jim go strip clubbing. Okay, what are we seeing here?"

"I see dogs and smell poop. What are you getting from this?"

"All we know so far, is that the pet shop owner was attacked and the dog was taken, along with money from the safe. I can see the robbery angle there, using the dog as bait, but here it was just dogs, no money, and they took the dogs at night. Of course, they would need the dogs to take and sell, then rob the store owners. Makes sense to me."

"But they got four dogs from here and six from the murder scene kennel. Then they took two from the dog show. Which was a stupid move. So that's twelve dogs, why so many if they're going to keep the dog after they rob the store owner? They could just use one good valuable dog for that." Buck said.

"True, why so many dogs?" Deacon's phone buzzed, he answered. "When did the call come in?" He listened, then said, "Okay, set it up and I'll be there." He hung up and turned to Buck. "One of the owners of a dog stolen from a kennel got a call. The voice on the phone asked for one hundred grand to return the dog."

"Damn, Jim was right. It was for ransom. What are we going to do now?"

"Warren is setting up a tap of the owner's phone. We need to go there."

They left with Buck following Deacon now. Deacon drove to the address Warren gave him on the phone. The house was on a nice street off Charleston. It had money written all over it. Deacon pulled up behind Warren's car and Buck slid in behind Deacon. They got out of their cars and went to the house. The techs from Electronics Division were in the dining room working their gadgets to tap the phone.

Warren went to Deacon. "The family called us when they got the call. Sorry to say, but the victim who was kidnapped was a dog and not a human. They love their animal, but called the police even though they were warned not to. They wanted this criminal caught."

Deacon was introduced to Mr. and Mrs. Lawson. "I'm sorry for your position in all this. May I ask why your dog was in the kennel?"

The man said, "We had the house fumigated. We also have two cats and they brought in fleas. We put the cats in a kennel that takes cats and the dog went to the Happy Puppy Kennel. We love our dog, but this is something I can't abide by. These men need to be arrested."

Kennel Murders

"Mr. Lawson, we'll do what we can to see that your dog is returned safely. Are you able to raise the money they asked for?"

"I'm rich, I have enough money to pay the ransom, but if we can get around it, I will. What good will all this do?" He motioned with a sweep of his hand to the techs hooking up their electronic gear.

"We'll see if we can get a fix on their location from the phone call and follow through to catch them." Deacon said.

"Just like on TV, before the police don't get a fix because the criminals also watch the TV to know how this works."

Deacon had no answer for the statement. It was true, TV crime shows gave away many things that would help the real police to track a criminal. It also showed criminals how to cover their crimes. A lot of bleach will clean blood from a crime scene. Many crimes have gone unsolved, because of the ways revealed by crime shows.

"You are quite right, but I hope these criminals don't watch too much TV," Deacon said as his cell phone buzzed. He excused himself and went into a hallway. Buck followed him out as Deacon was checking the caller ID. "It's Williams. I hope he has some good news from the pet shop." He answered.

Deacon listened for a few moments then hung up. He looked at Buck and said, "New mystery. They found a body out behind the pet shop, behind a dumpster. Shot in the back. Williams said the face on the body matches our sketch from the dog show. This is getting complicated."

"Maybe he's the one who tried to sell the dog to the pet store owner. But who killed him?"

"I don't know, but we have a mystery. I need to talk to Lawson again." Deacon went back into the room where everyone was waiting for a call. Deacon went to Lawson.

"Sir, what kind of dog was yours?"

"A Shar Pei. Very expensive breeding. We were grooming him for the big AKC dog shows," Lawson replied.

Deacon looked to Buck. "A Shar Pei. Sound familiar? There was only one on both our lists. It was the one in the pet shop and now it's being ransomed."

"I'm wondering if our dog thief tried to sell the dog without his buddies knowing. They found out when he went to get the money for the dog, murdered him and took the dog back. Now they're ransoming the mutt."

"That's as good a theory as any. Why else would our mystery thief be murdered behind the pet shop?"

*

Chapter 15

"Murder?" Lawson said. Deacon hadn't realized that they were standing close enough to the Lawsons for them to overhear his conversation with Buck.

"I'm sorry, there was a murder at the pet shop where your dog was being held, but it's missing again."

"How do you know it was our dog?"

Deacon paused, trying to find the best explanation. "Well, we got a call from a pet shop owner who said a sleazy looking man brought in a dog to sell. It was a Shar Pei. The store owner called us and we checked the dog. It had an ID chip and the owner of the kennel where you placed your dog identified the scan of the chip. It was the only Shar Pei taken from the kennels."

"But how did the criminals know it was our dog?"

"Each of the cages where they keep the dogs has a card attached with all the information about the dog and its owner. The fancier, well-bred dogs can be easily identified by anyone with any knowledge of dog breeds. I can't speak on the other crimes, including the murders, as we're still investigating. Now, if you could just concentrate on your dog and the phone call, we'll do what we can to catch a thief."

~~*~~

Penny was dressed and gathering her accessories to go out and take over the world. I was sitting in my wheelchair, starting to hate the thing, eating my toast. Willy was standing by Penny anticipating a trip.

"Where you off to on this sunny Saturday morning?" I asked.

"I'm meeting with Lynn and we are going to the second day of the dog show. We decided to just watch this time. I'm taking Willy so you'll have some privacy to work on your book."

"Very thoughtful of you. Just don't bring home any more dogs."

"Don't you want Willy to have a little playmate?"

"Turn him loose at the dog show to get his fill of other dogs. He'll be happy that he's an only child." I said with a grin.

Penny kissed me on the top of my head and put Willy in his purse. She picked up her car keys and said, "Don't get in trouble while I'm gone." She went out. I sat there in the silence of the house and then rolled out to the living room. I turned on the stereo, popped in a CD and played "Have to Believe We Are Magic" by Olivia Newton-John at full blast. I left the stereo playing as I went back to my home office to work.

~~*~~

Penny drove out to the Richards Investigating and Security office building where she had agreed to meet with Lynn. She pulled into the parking lot and went to the door. It was locked. She remembered it was Saturday and the office was closed, so she took out her key and let herself in. Lynn was in the lobby looking at the Review-Journal newspaper and smiled when she saw Penny in the outer lobby.

Penny came through the glass doors and said, "Good morning, are you ready for a day of dog watching, then a little shopping?"

"Ready, willing, and have money. I hit Deacon up this morning before he went off to catch a dognapper." She reached over and scratched Willy's head sticking out of the carrier. "All set to go when you are. Trapper's in his office, working on something. I'll let him know we're leaving." She went into the hallway to the offices while Penny waited.

The front door opened, startling Penny. She turned to see a woman entering the main lobby. "Are you open?" The woman asked.

"Actually, we're not, but can I help you?" Penny said, realizing she forgot to re-lock the front entrance.

The woman stood staring at Penny with a puzzled expression. "Aren't you Penny Wickens? From the TV?"

Penny chuckled and said, "Yes, I am, but this firm is owned by my husband, Jim Richards. He's home recuperating from an injury. Do you need help?"

"I do, I have a problem and I need help."

Lynn was re-entering the lobby from the offices and saw the woman. Penny turned and said, "We have a client."

Lynn came forward holding her hand out, "Lynn DeAngelo, investigator. How can we help you?"

"I'm Valerie Lyon, nice to meet both of you. Well, it's not some big crime, but someone took my dog," she said, and saw Willy. "Oh, you have your dog with you, he's so cute. I've seen him with you on your show."

"Thank you. Now explain about your missing dog," Penny said.

"Oh, yes. I had Victor in his dog run outside of our house and when I went out to get him, he was gone. The gate was still closed, so someone had to have taken him. I was going to take him to the dog show at the MGM Grand. He's entered in the competition."

"What kind of dog was he?" Lynn asked.

"A Cocker-Spaniel, full breed and registered with the AKC. He's valuable in the sense of future breeding. I know the police wouldn't bother trying to find him, what with the human crime in the city already. I looked in the phone book and found your agency."

Lynn looked at Penny, "Sounds like a pro-bono to me."

Penny grinned and agreed. She looked back to the woman and said, "I'm not sure what we can do at this time. You haven't had any calls for a ransom?"

"No. Nothing. No calls or note left to say they wanted money. You think they may call?"

"Not sure at this time. Give me your contact information and address. We can follow you home and if you have a photo of your dog, it would help." Lynn handed the woman a note pad from the front counter and she wrote her information down.

"Okay, you head home and we'll follow." Lynn said, and they all left the lobby heading to the front parking lot. Penny followed the woman out in her car, with Lynn in the passenger seat.

"Think we can find the pooch?" Penny asked Lynn as they drove.

"I hope so, but I'm not getting my hopes too high. That's why I said it would be a pro-bono case. No sense in charging for something we may not be able to solve. Her dog may be part of this crime wave of dognappings. I'm really curious to know what's going on." Lynn's phone buzzed, caller ID said it was Deacon, and she answered. "Hey, how's your case going?" She listened for a bit, explained about the dog missing from the home and then finished the call.

"This is getting stranger," Lynn said and covered what Deacon had told her. "He was surprised about this dog being taken from a home. He's got two murders to solve now, and still find the dogs. I know he doesn't like trying to solve cases, but since he became lieutenant, he's been a little more enthused about going to work."

"I can understand the thefts at the kennels and sort of understand the thefts at the dog show, but now they are stealing right from the homes." Penny said.

"Well, I'm thinking this theft may not be related to the crime wave. I think it was just someone stealing a dog from a backyard. But, I could be wrong."

They arrived at the house and got out. Lynn went to the woman and asked, "Just out of curiosity, have you boarded your dog in a kennel lately?"

"As a matter of fact, yes. My husband and I went on a flight to Cancun. We couldn't take the dog, so we put him in a kennel. It was hard to do, but it was the only solution."

"What kennel did you put him in?" Penny asked.

"Happy Puppy Dog Kennel," she replied.

Lynn and Penny looked at each other and smiled.

*

Chapter 16

Lynn excused herself and went off to the side of the yard. She pulled her phone and called Deacon.

"Hey, big boy, I got an update since our last call. It seems that the dog stolen from the Lyon's home is linked to the Happy Puppy Dog Kennel. Mrs. Lyon said they had their dog in the kennel this last month. Now it's gone. Do you think there could be an inside person in Happy Puppy giving info to the dognappers so they can go grab these expensive dogs for ransom?" She listened and then said she'd call if she got any more info.

Lynn came back to Penny and said, "It seems there has been a rash of ransom calls in the last hour.

Eight of the dogs that were taken are being ransomed."

"How could they arrange for the payoff of all those dogs without being caught?" Penny asked.

"Deacon said the criminals had given the victims a number to transfer money to an off-shore account. As were the other seven victims. They don't even have to pick up the money on the street. Deacon is trying to track down the transfer account, but it won't be easy. The off-shore banks aren't friendly enough to give info to anyone without an account password."

"I remember when Jim and I had to go down to a bank in the Cayman Islands to retrieve an account for the mistress murderer. They don't cooperate unless you have a pin number." Penny said.

"Well, the dognappers are using that ploy to collect the money." Lynn said.

Mrs. Lyon was bringing a picture of her dog to Lynn just as she heard her phone ringing in the house and excused herself. She went back inside while Penny and Lynn waited. About two minutes later she came back out looking upset.

"The person on the phone said if I wanted to see my dog again, I'd have to pay one hundred thousand dollars to them. I don't have that kind of money. I told them, but they said they would call with the information and hung up. I don't know what to do. Victor is our beloved dog, but I can't agree to pay that much money to get him back. I don't have it. If it were a child, I'd see if I could raise the money, but not a dog."

Penny thought about Willy, looking at the puppy sticking his head out of the purse. She had plenty of money and would do what she could to get Willy back if he were taken. But she could understand the logic behind the woman's problem.

"I need to ask, did your dog have an ID chip implanted?" Lynn asked the woman.

"Of course, it's the only way to identify our dog if he gets lost," she said, then started to cry. "I'm sorry, but Victor is like a child to us. I have to call my husband about this. Excuse me."

Lynn yelled to her, "We will be back. We have to investigate."

The woman waved them off, so Lynn and Penny went back to the car.

"Where are we going?" Penny asked.

"To see Deacon."

"I need to take a little side trip." Penny said as they got into the car.

Forty minutes later they got back into the car. "Doesn't that hurt the dog?" Lynn said as they left the vet's office parking lot.

"It's no worse than a flu shot," Penny replied. She set Willy on the back seat of the car. He didn't look happy. "Jim and I never thought to have a chip put in Willy. The last couple days made the decision for me. I need to know if this is my dog if he gets taken."

"I don't think he's agreeable to the procedure," Lynn said looking at the dog.

"It only hurts for a short time. He'll be better for it. Now we can go see Deacon."

As they drove, Lynn said, "I think your vet has a crush on you."

"Dr. Harris is in his twenties, he's too young for me," she said, then paused. "But, it's nice to think I still got it to make a young man like me."

"How are you and Jim doing? Still got the flame going?"

"I love Jim very much. He may not be perfect, but that's what makes him who he is. He makes me laugh with his little goof ups. Sometimes I think he does it deliberately. He cares about my problems and is always there to comfort me. He may not be the hunkiest man around, but he's my hunk."

"Deacon is like a child sometimes, but that's his way. I think that's what attracted me to him."

"Deacon is so funny at times with the way he lumbers around. He's like Big Bird," Penny said.

Lynn laughed out loud and agreed.

Deacon was standing outside the Lawson's home with Greg Warren, talking about the situation.

"I called in to the computer guys to see if they can locate the account of these criminals. But even with a court order, we may not be able to get the info. The banks are out of federal jurisdiction, let alone ours. We just have to wait and see what happens," Deacon said.

"But if the people do send their money to the account, will that guarantee the safe return of the dogs?" Warren asked.

"Won't know until it happens. One of the owners asked the dognapper about it and was told after the money is transferred they would be told where they could pick up their dog." Deacon paused to think. "You know, with that many dogs, they'd have to feed them. Maybe I should put a detail out to see if anyone has purchased large amounts of dog food."

"Deacon, think about how many places there are to buy dog food. Supermarkets, party stores, even gas stations. You'd have the whole force hunting the valley for places to get dog food."

"Well, it was a thought," Deacon said with a grin.

Penny's car had pulled up to the house and the women got out. Penny put Willy on his leash so he could relieve himself. Lynn went to the men.

Penny took the plastic glove from her pocket, lifted the dog poop, and folded the glove over it. She went to put it in the dog purse and found the one from the dog show yesterday. She smiled at forgetting to take it out. She was glad it didn't smell. She put the new one in and zipped the pouch back up, then went over to her friends.

"How's Jim feeling, Penny?" Deacon asked.

"Cranky, but lovable. I think he'll be more careful climbing ladders in the future," Penny replied.

Deacon's phone buzzed and he answered. "Who?" He paused. "That's great, do you have an address?" Another pause. "Thanks, text it to me." He hung up.

"Seems the people who killed our mystery man at the pet shop forgot that we could finger print him. They finally got an ID. He's Karl Hotchkiss and I got his address." He turned to Warren and said, "Stay with the Lawsons and see what develops. Call me with any news. I got a crime scene to check." He looked at Lynn and Penny and said, "Feel like tagging along?"

*

Chapter 17

Deacon called for back-up to the address he received in the text. He looked in the rearview mirror and saw that the women were still following behind him. He was going to be cautious when he arrived at the house. He didn't want his wife or their friend to be harmed. Even though Lynn was once his superior officer, he wasn't going to risk her life now. She was the mother of his beautiful daughter, so protecting her was his priority.

They pulled down the street in question and stopped just down from the house. The back-up arrived and waited for Deacon to take lead. The warrant showed up and Deacon got out of his car. When everyone gathered around him, he said, "I have no idea if this place has the dog theft ring, so we will go in assuming it is. Be careful of the dogs if they are in the building, humans are fair game. If they shoot, do what you're trained to do. Let's go."

They all moved swiftly down the street. Luckily, it was deserted and there were only a couple houses nearby. They all ran up to the front door and Deacon banged on it yelling, "Police, open up." Then he signaled for the ram to knock the door in. Once the opening was established, they all streamed into the house.

The men all went different directions and were calling out the clear signal. Deacon stood in the hallway and listened. He could hear dogs barking from somewhere in the house. One of the men called to him and Deacon went into the kitchen where the officer was pointing to a door. It went to the basement.

Deacon had a couple SWAT men take the lead down the stairs and when they established it was safe, he went down. It was a mess and stunk from dog droppings. He went to a big cage and counted seven dogs. The missing dogs weren't all there.

He turned back to the stairs and saw Lynn and Penny looking at the scene. He yelled, "Call Buck and have him get that woman from the kennel over here to identify these animals."

~~*~~

Buck had turned down my stereo so he could hear himself think. I came wheeling out to see who was messing with my music.

"How did you get in? Why didn't I hear the driveway alarm?" I asked.

"Well, your music was so loud you couldn't hear the alarm and I used the key you put out under that fake rock for me in case I had to get in." he said with a grin.

"Oh, that makes sense. I was working on my book." I said, sheepishly.

"It's nice, warm, and sunny out. Want to get out of the house?"

I thought for a couple seconds and then said, "Sounds like a winner. I'll get ready. Hold on." I drove the chair into my bedroom.

Buck was standing at my snack bar when his cell phone buzzed. Caller ID said it was Lynn. "Hey girl, what's up?" He listened and then grabbed a pad of paper on the snack bar and wrote something down. I was now back in the living room watching him and then he hung up.

"What's going on?" I asked.

"Lynn called and said they found a bunch of missing dogs and she wants me to get Volstad over there to ID the animals."

"Then get me in the van and we'll go." I headed for the door and Buck opened it for me. He had the ramp set up on the van. I guess he figured I would go out. I wheeled up the ramp and then he folded it to put in the van. He got in the driver's seat and called the kennel to talk to Volstad. He explained the situation and said he'd meet her at the house. He hung up and started the van.

"Got the directions to where we're going?" I asked.

Buck sat for a moment. "Okay, I have no idea where this place is."

I pulled my Android Samsung Note 2 phone and said, "Give me the address." He did. I punched the numbers into the phone's map program and it gave me the location. I said to get moving over to Charleston.

We arrived about ten minutes later and saw the house was surrounded by cops and forensics. Buck said that Valstad was there. He helped me out of the van and I told him to go to her. I sat in the chair feeling helpless watching the flurry of activity. I knew I couldn't go into the house with this chair, so I waited.

I saw Penny coming out of the house and waved to her. She came over to me.

"Buck said you were out here. Sorry you can't stick your nose into this," she said with a grin. She explained what was found in the house. "The kennel woman is checking out the dogs. She says that those four are from her kennel."

"How does she know that?"

"She brought a clipboard with a list of the dogs and a scanner to read their chips. She is writing down the information of the three other dogs that probably came from the other kennel, where the employee was murdered."

Kennel Murders

"So if they found seven dogs here that means six are still out there, not counting the two taken from the dog show." I looked toward the house as animal control was bringing out the dogs. "The ones that are still missing, are they the ones being ransomed?"

"I don't know, but I'm sure Deacon will have that information after the kennel lady gets done."

Buck came back to us and smiled. "Well, we're getting somewhere. CSI is tearing the place apart and finding all kinds of good things. There was a message on his antique answering machine from some guy named Bernie asking Hotchkiss to bring the next dog to the shop. What shop, he didn't say. They're doing a trace on the call."

"Any word on the ransom dogs?" I asked.

"Valstad said that two more calls for money came in." Buck said. "The people who put the now missing dogs in her kennel aren't happy. I hope she doesn't get sued because of the thefts and ransom demands. I'm going to do my best to help get them back. I also want to take a bite of ass from each of these guys behind this. Humans are fine for kidnapping, but helpless dogs shouldn't be subjected to this."

"You're a pit bull, Buck. I'll bet you could take a big chunk of butt from these guys. I guess there's not much now until they trace the call." I said.

"Nope, Deacon said they'd be on it shortly." Buck said.

"Did someone mention my name?" Deacon said as he came up with Lynn.

"Are you a dognapper?" Penny asked.

"Not since I was a kid" Lynn smacked him on the arm. "Hey, I was kidding," Deacon defended.

"The subject is touchy right now. At least until we find the killer or killers of the kennel employee and Hotchkiss." Lynn said. "These people aren't just dog thieves, they're murderers now."

*

Chapter 18

"Any word on the phone trace?" I asked.

"Not yet. As soon as they get a fix on it, they'll let me know." Deacon said. "Must be a bitch stuck in that chair?"

"I think he should just stay home," Penny said.

"Jim stay home? I hardly think so," Bucked mugged. "He'll be eating the wallpaper."

"He could set up a bedroom in the office and camp out there," Lynn chimed it.

"Thanks, everyone. Now, are you finished?" I replied.

"Sorry, sweetie, you are just so helpless that it's fun." Penny said.

"Oh, I can't fight back, is that what it is?" I said.

Someone called to Deacon from the house. He turned and left us.

"I'm going to follow him," Lynn said and went off.

"So Jim, you want to hang in here or I could take you to the dog show?" Buck said.

"You need to investigate the theft of dogs, so I go where you go." I replied. "I don't think I could drive the van with a cast on."

"Well, I'll find out what Deacon has and we can go." Buck went to the house, leaving Penny and me alone.

"Did you want to go to the dog show, sweetie?" Penny said. "You can get into my car and I can put your chair in the trunk."

"Babe, do you know how heavy this chair is? You'd break your back lifting it. I appreciate the offer, but you'd have to drive the van to take me anywhere. I know you don't like driving the van."

"Well, I offered," she said.

"And I appreciate it. I'm going to have Buck take me back to the house and I'll go into my home office and write. You're on your own."

Deacon, Lynn and Buck came back to us.

"The phone was a burner. They can't get a fix on it, so we don't have any idea where to go from there. But CSI got some prints from the house and they are going to run them. They got quite a few, so it may take a while. We still may have a lead." Deacon said.

"Are you going to follow up on the link between the woman whose dog was taken from her home and the fact that she had the dog in the Happy Puppy Kennel?" Penny asked.

"Sure, it's something. If our dognappers took her dog, they'd have to know where she lived." Deacon turned to Lynn. "Would it be an imposition to ask you to follow up on that?"

"Bunny bear, I'd be glad to investigate." Lynn turned to Penny. "Care to join me?"

Penny looked to me. I said, "Go investigate. I'll be at home making money writing."

She kissed my forehead and handed me Willy. He plopped down on my lap and I said, "Don't forget us now."

Penny gave Lynn the high five and they went back to the house. Deacon smiled and said, "You shouldn't have turned her loose like that. Lynn will lead her down the path of crime-fighting."

"As if she doesn't get enough hanging around me," I said. "Buck, take me home and go play detective."

Buck helped wheel me back into the van. I looked out to Deacon and said, "Keep an eye on the women. Don't want them getting into trouble since I'm disabled and can't save them."

Buck laughed and closed the door on me. Deacon waved to me through the window as Buck got in to drive away. Deacon stood watching us drive off.

~~*~~

Penny and Lynn got back to the house to find Ms. Valstad. The woman was watching Animal Control carefully putting the dogs into cages on their truck. She had given them directions to her kennel where she would call the owners to come and retrieve their pets.

"Ms. Valstad," Lynn called as they came up.

The woman turned to see them coming. "I'm so glad we got most of the dogs back. I hope they can find the others."

Kennel Murders

"I need to ask a question. Do you know a woman named Valerie Lyon?"

Valstad look like she was trying to remember the name. "It's familiar, but I can't place it."

"She had her dog in your kennel last month. A Cocker Spaniel."

"Ah, yes. Now I remember. People's names are sometimes too hard to remember, but dogs, I don't forget. What about her?"

"The dog was taken from her yard and she mentioned that the dog had been boarded at your kennel recently. Seems like a coincidence that her dog was taken. I'm wondering if one of your employees could have given information to the dognappers about Lyon's dog and where she lived."

"I hope you're not insinuating that my people would be part of this dreadful crime," Valstad said indignantly.

"Just trying to piece together leads to help find the culprits involved. I'd like to talk to your people to see what they have to say."

Valstad was silent for a moment. "I guess if it would help to clear my people. Feel free to talk to them if you must. I'm going back to the kennel with the dogs and call their owners. You can join me there."

Lynn agreed and watched the woman give further instructions to the Animal Control officer to find the Kennel. Then she went to her car.

Lynn looked to Penny and said, "Shall we go, Watson?"

"On the trail, Sherlock." They went to Penny's car and followed Valstad out.

They drove a short while through the streets of Vegas until they came to the kennel. Lynn parked in the side lot of the party store next to the kennel. She didn't want to get in the way of the Animal Control now unloading the dogs. Lynn was glad that Deacon had the officers come in to help take the dogs to the kennel.

Lynn and Penny came up to the back door where the dogs were being put into the cages in the back room of the building. They stood watching as the poor, tired looking dogs were given a better place to rest. Valstad was putting dog food into their cages and the dogs took to it as though they hadn't eaten in days.

The officers of Animal Control left and Lynn stood with Penny watching the dogs eat. Valstad was on the phone at a desk on the side of the pleasant room. She was starting to call the owners of the recovered dogs. She had finished and came back to the women.

"I've got a lot of relieved people who will be in to get their dogs. I'm going to lose money on this, but hopefully I won't be sued," Valstad said.

They heard a familiar voice at the door from the front of the building, it was Buck. "How's the pups?" he asked as he entered the room.

Valstad smiled and said, "They all look healthy so far. I'm recommending, to the owners, a vet I know. I'll have to pay for the check-ups for the animals, it was my responsibility to take care of them."

"How many of these dogs were ransomed?" Buck asked.

"None of these dogs were. The ones that are still missing are the victims of ransom."

"So, they are being held somewhere unknown?" he asked. She agreed. Buck looked to Lynn and Penny and said, "Shall we talk to the employees here and see if they might know where the missing dogs are."

*

Chapter 19

Valstad had all of the four employees come to the back room so Buck and Lynn could question them. She then went to the front to wait for the dog owners. Since neither Buck nor Lynn were police, they had to handle this carefully.

"I'm Lynn DeAngelo and this is Buck Carter. We're private investigators hired to find out who took the dogs from this kennel and Paradise Kennel. We'd like to ask you a few questions to help us in our investigation."

None of the three women and one man objected, so Lynn took two of them and gave the other two to Buck. Penny sat back in a chair watching Lynn work.

"Now you are?" she asked the two women with her.

"I'm Lori Riggs," one said. The other said, "Marge Jokenen."

"Lori, we have information that a dog, which had been boarded here within the last month, was recently taken from a private home. It was a valuable Cocker Spaniel owned by Valerie Lyon. Is that name familiar?" Lynn watched their faces to see any hint of familiarity. The woman named Lori looked down at the floor, unsmiling. Marge gladly said she didn't remember the name.

"Marge, you can go back up front to help Valstad. Lori, stay here please."

Marge left and Lynn took Lori to a chair by a desk. "Please sit."

Lori was avoiding looking at Lynn.

"I'll be right back," Lynn said. "Don't move."

Lynn went to Buck, who had just finished talking to the man and woman.

"Anything from them?" she asked.

"Nah, they're clueless. I believe them. They don't know anything."

"I got one over here who may be in on it." Lynn turned back and went to the woman, with Buck following.

Buck whispered to Lynn, "Just like back in interrogation." Buck went over to Penny, still watching.

Lynn smiled and sat on a chair by the woman. "So, Lori, you say you don't know about the missing dog from the Lyon's home?"

The woman didn't look at Lynn, just continued looking to the floor.

"Lori!" Lynn yelled, startling everyone in the room. "Look at me!"

Lori's head snapped up, her face giving a frightened expression to Lynn.

"You know something about the dog being taken from Valerie Lyon, don't you?" she said quietly, but still forcefully.

Lori still didn't speak.

"If you know about the dognapping at Lyon's house, then you know about the dogs taken from the kennels. And maybe you know about the murder of the employee at the Paradise Kennel?"

Lori still didn't speak.

"If you are in this, then you will be charged with accessory to murder and you will get the same punishment the killer gets. Could be life in prison or even the death penalty."

That got a response from Lori. "I didn't have anything to do with the killing. I don't know who did that, honestly!" She was in a panic now. "I just followed orders, that's all!"

"Orders? Who's orders?"

"I don't know, I got a phone call and the voice on the phone said that they would kill my boyfriend, Derek, if I didn't do what they say. I thought they had Derek hostage. I asked what they wanted me to do and the voice said to give them names and addresses of people with expensive dogs. I named about four owners and then the caller hung up. Derek wasn't kidnapped, he was in our apartment, safe. I'm so sorry."

Lynn didn't speak, taking a moment to think, then she said, "Do you remember who the other dog owners were?"

Lori paused and she said, "I can write them down for you."

"Good," Lynn said and turned to the desk, finding a piece of paper and a pen, handing them to Lori. "Give me those names."

"Oh, I don't know them by heart, but I could get them from the computer for you."

Lynn stood and said, "Get to it."

Lori stood and went to the computer on the desk and began typing. About five minutes later she printed out the name of four families, including Valerie Lyon. She handed the sheet to Lynn.

"Okay, this will help your case." She handed the sheet to Buck and said, "Get this to Deacon, these people need to be watched."

Buck stood and left the room. Lynn turned to Penny. "Shall we go grab something to eat?"

Lori spun in the chair, "What about me?"

"You can get your own food," Lynn said.

"No, I mean about my involvement in the murder?"

"Oh, yes. I'll talk to the D.A. and see what we can work out. But I wouldn't sweat it. You helped us and I'll remember that. Now go back to work and don't leave town."

The girl jumped up and left the room. Lynn and Penny were going through the door to the front when they saw someone familiar. Ray Zink. He was standing at the counter talking to Valstad.

"Mr. Zink, how are you?" Lynn called out to him. He looked surprised.

"I'm fine. I just stopped here to see how the case was going. I was just asking if they found the person I identified." Zink said, composing himself.

"I don't think Ms. Valstad would know that information. You should have called Detective DeAngelo at LVMPD. It was his case."

"Yes, I agree. I just thought since the dogs were taken from here, Ms. Valstad would know."

"Well, she wouldn't and didn't until we told her earlier."

"Sorry, I wasn't thinking. I thought she may know since the crimes were connected. Well, I have to go back to work. Thanks for the information."

"Mr. Zink, did you know the man you identified was murdered?"

He stopped and looked surprised. "No, I didn't know that."

"Yes, he was murdered behind the Friendly Pets Store. He was the man you ID'd at the convention center."

"I'm sorry to hear that. Do you have any leads to his killer?"

"We think it may have been his own people. We think he was trying to sell an expensive dog to the pet shop, but the dog is now missing. We don't have much to go on, other than your identifying him."

"Well, I did what I could do. Now if you'll excuse me, I'm getting late for work."

"It's afternoon, do you start your day at work late?"

"I was on a lunch break." He was starting to act nervous.

"Where do you work, Mr. Zink?" Lynn asked.

"Uh, I work for a sporting goods company. I'm a sales person. Now I really have to leave."

"Just give me the name of the sporting goods company and you can go."

He hesitated, "I don't want the company to know that I was involved in a crime."

"Oh, we'll be discreet. What company?"

"Outdoor Sports. On Maryland."

"Thank you, Mr. Zink. We'll be in touch." Lynn smiled as the man turned to the door and left quickly.

"That was odd," Buck said.

"Yes, quite a coincidence that he came here. I'll talk to Deacon and have him follow up on Zink. He may be a person of interest." She then looked at Buck and said, "Did you get the names to Deacon?"

"Yep, he's already assigning surveillance teams to the three addresses left on the list.

Lynn looked over to Ms. Valstad. "How well do you know that man?"

"Not very well. He boarded his dog here once, that's all I know about him."

"If he comes back again, let me know what he wanted." Lynn handed her a business card, then turned to Buck and Penny. "Nothing more here to do, shall we go get food?"

*

Chapter 20

~~*~~

Deacon was back at the precinct explaining about the kennel murder case to Captain Weber. Deacon had hoped to avoid the man, but he always popped up unexpectedly when you weren't looking.

"So, you've put officers on the homes where the dogs may be taken from?" Weber asked.

"I'm hoping we can nab one live dognapper. Through him we may find the dogs being ransomed."

"One hundred thousand dollars for a dog. That's a bit excessive." Weber said. "Back when I was a lieutenant, we had a series of dognappings and the top price was two thousand dollars. We were told back then it was the going rate for well-bred dogs."

"Criminals are getting greedy. And owners of fancy animals have more money these days."

"True. It cost money to breed and groom a dog for shows today. It's big business now," Weber said. "Well, do what you can. Is Lynn helping at all?"

"Yes, sir. She's checking on the dogs at the first kennel that was hit. She was hired by a woman whose dog was taken from a backyard."

"Has Richards check in on this?"

"No, sir. He's been disabled from a fall. Broke his leg."

"Ouch, that's not good for a man of his age. Bones get brittle."

"A fall from five feet up can do some damage for any age, if they hit the ground just right."

"True. Well, go to it, I'll leave you alone. Oh, and keep expenses down on the surveillance if you can. Our budget is shrinking."

"Yes, sir," Deacon said, as he breathed easier while Weber walked away.

Warren was standing behind Deacon and said, "What are we doing now?"

"The waiting game, as always. Go check with forensic and see if they got anything from the prints off the house. I need to check with Lynn to see what she has."

Greg Warren went off and Deacon went to his office— formerly Lynn's office. He sat and dialed Lynn's number. After a few rings Lynn answered.

"Hey bunny bear, how's things going?" Lynn said.

"You know I've asked you before not to call me bunny bear." Deacon grumbled.

"You said not to call you that in front of your men. Are you in front of your men?"

"Not at the moment. But if you keep it up, you'll slip and do it in front of my men. How can I maintain authority if my men think of me as bunny bear?"

"It's cute and so are you. What's happening?"

"Nothing cute. I just explained to Weber what was going down. He's unusually friendly, it worries me."

"Probably because I'm not there. I don't think he likes women in command."

"Whatever, he seems sneaky lately. I don't have much more to tell you. Anything good from the kennel?"

"Other than what I had Buck pass on to you. Oh, wait. Remember Zink, the guy who ID'd the dognapper at the dog show? He turned up at the kennel, acting sneaky. It must be spreading."

"Did he have an excuse for being there?" Deacon asked.

"He said he was checking to see if we found the criminal who took the dog. I'm suspicious that he showed up there. Since we found out that one of the employees gave out information about dog owners, he turns up. Can you run a background check on him? You should still have his info. He said he works at Outdoor World on Maryland."

"I'll have Warren track him down when he gets back. He's checking on the prints from the house. I'm wearing down and there have been no more calls about the ransom of the dogs. They just stopped. I'm wondering if the dognappers are changing their minds or direction."

"Whatever, I'll see you back at the apartment. I have to pick up the baby from here."

"Give her a kiss for me." Deacon said.

"You kiss her yourself, we'll be home shortly. See you then," she said and hung up.

Bob Moats

Deacon sat back as Warren entered the office. "Anything?"

"Yeah, every print came back to members of a gang out of LA. Each one has a number of records including dog theft. Guess they moved to the rich part of the world."

"I'd say LA has more rich, spoiled stars who love their dogs. But if they all have records, they had to cool it in tinsel town. Okay, I need you to check on our man who ID'd the criminal at the dog show, Ray Zink. Check his background, financials, phone calls if you can. Anything to give us a take on whether he's in on this."

"I'll get right on it," Warren said and went out.

~~*~~

I was busy at my computer desk typing out my story about the murders of lawyers and the kingpin of crime, Alphonse Grisler. The shyster lawyer who hired me to find someone who wanted to murder him. Too bad he lived. I looked over to the small monitor on my desk that was hooked wirelessly to cameras around the house. I could see Penny drive into the garage and park.

Kennel Murders

I hit the control on my wheelchair and rolled out of the room. Willy was on my trail, nipping at the wheels. I had to be careful not to roll over him, so I reached down and picked him up. Penny was coming into the kitchen as I came through the door.

"Hi, sweetie. Have a good day writing?"

"Yep, almost finished with the book. I can start my next after this one is edited and double checked." .

Penny picked up Willy from my lap and hugged him. "I've seen so many dogs today, I'm glad ours is small."

"Did you eat?" I asked.

"Yes, Lynn, Buck and I went out to eat. We had steak to celebrate our good day investigating."

"You caught the dognappers?"

She covered what had gone on today as I listened. "And now they need to catch one of the dognappers stealing from someone's yard."

"Yes, it sounds like a good day of investigating. Now can you feed me? I can't reach the food in the fridge or reach the microwave."

"Such a baby. You know you can stand on that cast, don't you?"

"But it's more fun if you feed me," I said with a grin.

She kissed the top of my head and said, "Then starve." She took Willy and left the kitchen.

I yelled, "You are a mean woman. I'm leaving you out of my will!" I knew she had more money than I did, from her show, but she could live so much better with what I had from my book sales.

I could hear her laughing down the hall as I rolled back out to the living room. I drove over to the remote for the TV and turned it on. Then I reached into the small cooler I had Buck set up with Pepsi and ice before he left. I pulled out a bottle and relaxed, watching television, waiting for Penny to come back out.

*

Chapter 21

Monday morning came fast and every one was up and ready to work. Everyone except me. I didn't feel like getting up and told Penny so.

"Are you going to use this accident to get lazy now?" she said as she got ready to go tape her show. "I'm not accepting your weak excuses. You're capable of moving, so do so."

I tried to bury my head in the pillow just as she pulled it off me. "Don't even think about going back to sleep. If I have to go to work, you do, too."

"Buck is busy." I said.

"No, he's in the driveway getting the ramp set up for you. I told him to take you to the office and make sure you wait until I get there after my show. You stay there or I'll divorce you."

I looked up at her and said, "Yes, dear."

She left to go to her station and Buck was helping me to my chair after I managed to get dressed.

"How much longer are you in this cast, Jim?" Buck asked.

"I get to have the cast removed next week, and then I get a walking cast. Although I think I'll keep using the chair."

"You think it's a good idea to keep using the chair?"

"No, but I like it. Now, can we go?"

"You're the boss man," Buck said and opened the front door as I zipped out.

Twenty minutes later, we were at the office building and I entered the back door, almost running over Earl.

"You still using that thing? I figured you'd be running around by now," Earl said.

"One more week and I'll at least be up and standing. Anything going on here?"

"It's been peaceful while you've been gone. Trapper is out with Sam, they're still trying to get the magic back."

"Maybe he's using the wrong magic, or his wand may not have enough power," I said with a grin.

Buck groaned and said, "I have to go to the kennel to see if the dogs were returned to their owners and how many of the others paid the ransom."

"I can't see people paying a hundred grand for a dog," Earl said.

"Have you ever owned a dog?" I asked.

"I have, and I loved that dog, but I wouldn't go as far as a hundred grand."

"How far would you go?" Buck asked.

"I'd negotiate the price. Try to get it down to a couple grand."

"These people don't negotiate. They murdered two people, they don't care for your negotiations."

"When I speak, they will negotiate," Earl said, with a growl.

I believed that with his skills he could get them to change their demands.

"Why don't you help Deacon with his case?" I asked.

"I'm not getting in Lynn's way, she's already marked her territory on this."

"You're talking like she's a dog," I said.

"Whatever. I've got investigating to do." He made an evil laugh and went down the hallway to his office.

"I've got to go," Buck said. "I'll be back later to take you home." He left us and went out the back door.

I was left alone, so rolled up to the front lobby to see what Lacey was up to. I went through the glass doors to the front and came around the side so Lacey could see me. She wasn't at her desk. I looked around the best I could from my vantage point below the rest of the world. I rolled around the desk and to the door leading to the new addition and lounge I had put in. I drove into the lounge and found Lacey and Tracey playing foosball.

"Hey!" I yelled, and they both screamed. Great, now I was scaring both of them.

"What are you doing?" Lacey challenged.

"Making sure that my employees are doing their jobs. What if someone comes in to hire us?"

Lacey pointed to a small box on a table nearby. "It's a receiver for the front door. If someone comes in, I'll know."

"Okay, I'll give you that. But what about your reports?"

"They're all done. So ease up, we're relaxing."

I smiled and said, "Have fun." I steered my chair out of the room as I heard the sound of the ball being hit by plastic men's feet.

I went to my office and pulled up to my desk. I picked up the remote control and turned on the TV. It didn't go on.

"What the hell?" I said and reached for the phone and punched the button for Lacey. I guess she could hear the phone from the lounge, she answered. "What!"

"Something's wrong with my TV." I said.

"No, it's unplugged," she said.

"And may I ask why?"

"Penny's orders, don't ask." Then she hung up.

Great, now I was trapped in my office building and couldn't watch my TV. I rolled out to the front lobby and tried to turn on the TV in the waiting area. It didn't work either. "Not fair," I mumbled, and turned to the front window to look out to the Vegas skyline. It was something that always entertained me.

"I guess I'll just have to meditate until Penny gets here."

~~*~~

Deacon and Buck entered the back room at the kennel and found Ms. Valstad standing by a cage with a man and a woman. They were taking a dog out of a cage and the woman was in tears. Deacon leaned to Buck and said, "Dog owners."

"At least it's a happy reunion," Buck said back.

Valstad saw Buck and Deacon and nodded. The men went off to the side and watched.

The man spoke. "I'm thankful our dog has been returned to us. Although I hold you responsible

153

for any upsetting terror our dog went through. We will be consulting our dog's therapist and see what she says. If the dog has been traumatized, we will take legal action."

Deacon was grumbling as the man spoke. He shook his head and went to the man. "Sir, you have your dog. Be happy. I'm amazed that you believe your animal needs therapy. Do you really think he understands anything that went on the last couple days? Are you so dense that you think this dog is traumatized by this? If you even think of coming back here with your petty problems, I'll see that your life is made miserable."

The man looked shocked and said, "Who are you?"

"I'm the police, and your worst nightmare, you got that?"

The man looked to his wife, who was holding the dog, he took her arm and they left quickly.

"Dipshit." Deacon let out a breath. "I hate dealing with people like them. Arrogant idiots." He turned to Valstad and said, "If he even comes back here, you call me."

She smiled and said, "Thank you, it's only the beginning. I may have to shut down after the lawsuits start coming in. These people think they are important because they have some money."

Deacon looked to the dogs still waiting to be picked up. "Maybe we should ransom the rest, just to take these people down a peg."

"It would be welcome. But I'm tired of dealing with these snobs, I may welcome closing down."

*

Chapter 22

"After I found out what happened with Lori, I was going to fire her, but your wife talked me out of it. The girl meant no harm. She was fooled into doing something she wouldn't have done otherwise if they hadn't threatened her boyfriend." Valstad said.

"These people are no fools. We don't have enough officers available to cover all the dog owners who are being threatened with ransom. Have you heard from any of the owners from your kennel about further calls?" Deacon asked.

"Just one, and they said they would pay, but only if the man brought the price down. The man on the phone said they'd think about it and hung up. They heard nothing more."

The office phone rang and Valstad excused herself. She went to answer then listened. She was silent then said, "The police detective who is in charge of that is here. Would you like to talk to him?" She listened then held the phone out to Deacon.

He took the phone and asked if it was a speaker phone, she said it was and pushed a button. Then Deacon said, "Detective DeAngelo, who am I speaking to?"

The voice came out of a box on the desk. "Michael Bosley, are you the person I should talk to?"

"I'm investigating the murder of a kennel employee, so it's part of my investigation to find these criminals. What is it you need?"

"My wife and I got a call from the dognappers saying that they would return my dog if I paid the ransom to their bank account. They did say they would lower the price to ten thousand dollars if I had the money in their account by three today."

"Why did you call this kennel?"

"I wanted to see if anyone else had the same offer. I wasn't going to pay ten grand if someone else was going to pay less."

"I'm sure you want your dog back, are you going to pay?"

"If that's the demand, I will. Have you heard from anyone else?"

"It's a little hard to coordinate all the dog owners since they are spread around the city. You're the first I've heard that had a lower offer. Where are you staying at?"

"We're in the Samuels Hotel until we get our dog back. It's too late for the dog show now, so we will be going back home to Arizona."

"Mr. Bosley, I'll be right over to see you, don't mention you talked to me if they call back. If you decide to pay, find out where they will release the dog to you. I'll be there shortly." Deacon hung up and said to Buck, "Let's go. Thanks, Ms. Valstad. I'll talk to you later."

Deacon and Buck left and drove to the hotel on the east end of Tropicana Avenue. The desk clerk was leery about giving out the Bosley's room number, but deacon showed his badge and said it was important. The clerk called up for an okay from Bosley and then told Deacon where the room was.

Deacon knocked at the door to the room and it was answered by a rather portly man standing about five-nothing. He was bald and had a full white beard, reminding Deacon of a mini Santa Claus.

"Mr. Bosley, I'm Detective DeAngelo. This man is a private investigator working for a victim of the dognappers. Have you had a call since I talked to you?"

"No, but we've been waiting to hear something. Come in please."

They went into the main area of the suite. It was very elegant looking, well-decorated with expensive knick-knacks and furniture. Deacon could understand why the hotel didn't allow pets in the rooms.

"How long ago did they call?" Deacon asked.

"Within the last hour. I'm hoping they call back soon. I've arranged for my bank to transfer the funds provided they are serious about decreasing the price. I'll go no higher."

There was a woman sitting on an easy chair and she sobbed when he said that. The man turned to her. "Doris, we've already discussed this. I know you love your dog, but that kind of money is out of the question." He looked back to Deacon. "I'm not being heartless, and if this were a child, I'd pay whatever they asked."

Deacon was watching the woman. "Mr. Bosley, there are a large number of people who consider their pets as their children. When you invest time and love into an animal for years it's hard not to think of them as children."

"Maybe so, but I have had no time to invest love into my wife's dog." He said that just as his room phone rang. He looked at Deacon and said, "It's probably them."

"Answer it and go ahead with the deal. Find out the exact details for returning the dog."

Bosley answered and listened. "I have the money ready for transfer, but I want to know if you are keeping your end of the deal by returning my wife's dog?"

He listened and said, "I'm not from Vegas, I don't know where that is." He listened as Deacon pulled the phone from Bosley's ear a little so he could hear.

The voice said, "The drug store is a Rite-Aid. On the corner of Flamingo and Spenser Street. Ask anyone for directions. When I get word that the money was deposited, the dog will be tied to the bottled water dispenser machine outside the front of the building. If the money isn't in my account by three, you'll get the dog back in pieces." The man hung up.

Deacon stood away from the man and pulled his cell phone out. He pushed buttons then listened. "Greg, we got a ransom demand and a report of a dog being returned." Deacon explained the situation then continued. "Get some undercover officers and cars at that Rite-Aid and watch to see who ties the dog up. Don't grab the person, just follow them to wherever they go and call me." He hung up and turned to Bosley.

"Go ahead and deposit the money. If we catch the criminals, you can put in a request to hopefully have your funds returned."

Bosley picked up his cell phone from a table and made a call. A couple minutes later the transaction was finished. He hung up and said, "Now what?"

"I guess we wait to see if they call about the transfer. Or, we can take you to the drugstore to recover your dog."

"Let's do that," Bosley said and helped his wife up.

"Do you have a car?" Deacon asked.

"Yes, we were close enough to drive here from Arizona. I'll follow you."

Everyone went out to the cars and Deacon drove over to Flamingo, going to the drugstore. Deacon's cell buzzed and he answered. "Yeah?" He listened and then hung up. He said to Buck, "Some man did tie the dog to the water dispenser machine and left. Two of our cars are following him. Warren said they'd give me a location when they find out where the perp is going."

"Mighty glad they did give the dog back." Buck said.

"I'm sure the Bosley's will be happy." Deacon said as they pulled into the parking lot of the Rite-Aid. They could see the dog tied to the machine. A couple of young boys were standing, looking at the dog, then one of the boys reached down to untie it. Deacon hit his sirens and lights, scaring the boys into running. Deacon and Buck laughed. They parked as Bosley pulled up, then Mrs. Bosley came flying out of their car and ran to the dog.

*

Chapter 23

"Mr. Bosley, you should come down to our precinct and file a complaint. So we have record that you paid the ransom." Deacon said.

"I'd just like to get out of town, and never come back here. Ten grand is a spit in the bucket for me, I'll just write it off on my taxes. We're going back to the hotel, pack and get the hell out of town. Thank you for whatever you did." He grabbed his wife's arm and led her to the car. They drove out as Buck and Deacon stood watching them go.

"Excitable, wasn't he?" Buck said.

"At least he didn't say he was planning to sue Valstad."

"Hopefully he doesn't change his mind." Buck chuckled and went to the car.

Deacon sat at the wheel, pulled his car radio's microphone, and called for Warren. "What's the progress on the perp?"

"He's going way out by Mount Charleston. We still have him in sight. I'll give you a yell when he lights somewhere." Warren replied.

"Just observe, don't move in until you let me know what the situation is. I'll get some more men out then."

"Got it," Warren said and clicked off.

"Now what?" Buck asked.

"I haven't heard anything from the Lawsons. Since they got the ransom call for their Shar Pei, nothing new has come in. Since Bosley paid, maybe they'll contact Lawson with a reduced offer." Deacon pulled his cell phone and made a call. "Williams, anything on the Lawson ransom demand?"

He clicked on the speaker so Buck could hear. "It's been quiet since you were last here. You think they may be changing direction again?" Williams said.

"We just got one dog back and are pursuing the perp who dropped the dog off. I'm waiting to hear from Greg on where they end up at. Tell the Lawsons that we may have a lead on the place where the dogs are being held and to hold off on paying. Just tell them not to answer the phone, that should baffle the crooks."

"Lawson is getting very antsy. I hope that satisfies him. I'll call if anything develops."

"Thanks, talk later," Deacon said and disconnected.

"Now we wait until Greg gives us a location." Deacon said to Buck. "We may as well go back to the precinct and organize from there."

Deacon started the car and drove back. They entered the building just as Weber came in the squad room. "Crap," Deacon said quietly.

"Deacon, got anything on the dognappers?"

"Yes, sir. Greg Warren is tailing the perp who dropped off one of the dogs about thirty minutes ago. He's heading up around Mt. Charleston. He'll call as soon as he gets a fix. If we can find their base of operations, we should be able to retrieve the rest of the dogs."

"Very good, DeAngelo. I knew you could handle this. Carry on," he said and zipped off out of the squad room.

Deacon looked at Buck, "That man is amazing. He pops in and out and I wonder if he really does anything."

Buck laughed, "Doesn't matter, he is the boss."

"That he is. Let's go get this operation in gear." They went to Deacon's office and Deacon called Warren.

His voice came over the box on Deacon's desk. "The perp is still traveling, but he's turned direction and is heading back to Vegas. I don't know if he knows we're following or suspects he might be followed. I suspect he's trying to lose us, or whoever he thinks may be following. This may take a while."

"Okay, let me know." They finished and disconnected.

~~*~~

I was in my office when Penny came bombing in. "Good, you're still awake." She smiled.

"Is that a good thing?" I asked.

"You bet, sweetie. I'm going to change your life."

That worried me. "Okay, how?"

"Hold on," she said and went out of the room. Willy was at my feet, so I picked him up and put him on my desk. He plopped down and snorted. "You are a lot of help. What's Mommy plotting?"

Lacey came into the room followed by Tracey. "What's Penny up to?" I asked them.

They stood silently. "We're not allowed to say." Lacey spoke solemnly.

"Well, this is disturbing," I said.

Trapper, followed by Earl, came in the room. "Now this is worrying me. Is this an intervention?"

Trapper grinned, "You're going to like it."

"What?" I said.

"Hold on, it's coming." Earl said.

I looked to the door as Penny and Lynn came in. Lynn stopped just outside the door. Penny came over to me and stood looking serious.

"Am I dying? Have you heard from the doctor who fixed my leg? Has he found something else?"

"Sweetie, be quiet. This is serious," she said, giving me a kiss on my head.

"Now I know I'm dying."

"No, we're here to help you. As you know, since you started investigating the classmate murders case, murder has followed you."

"Is this about the curse everyone says I have?"

"Yes, and I have a solution. Today on my show I had a guest who will break your curse."

"Break my curse? Are you serious? I don't have a curse."

"Well, then this shouldn't hurt." Penny turned to Lynn at the door and waved.

Lynn motioned to someone just outside of my view. Suddenly, a woman dressed in Gypsy garb, bright and wild, came around the corner and into the room. She had a look on her face that worried me.

"You!" she shrieked and pointed to me, I almost jumped out of the chair. "I can see the aura about you. The death curse! It emanates from you and spreads out to the ether!"

Okay, now I was trying not to laugh. I forced myself to look serious. She pulled out a stick decorated with feathers and bangles. She waved it in the air and spoke in a language I thought sounded

Jamaican. She danced around my chair, which was now in the middle of the room after Penny moved me. She was bopping and jiving, waving her stick and arms, chanting strange incantations. She came around and moved her face close to mine.

"I command the evil to release from this man. Death be gone!" she shrieked and then fell away from me. She hopped and danced some more, then ran from the room, yelling, "Death follow me! This man is purged now!"

I sat in amazement as she disappeared out of the room. Penny came to me and kissed my head again.

"Do you feel lighter now?" she asked.

I figured I better play along or Penny would never let me hear the end of this. "Oh, yes, I do feel so much better. Thank you for this." I was trying my hardest not to break out laughing.

I looked over to Trapper and Earl. I could tell they wanted to bust out laughing. Lynn was already holding her hand over her mouth, giggling. Tracey was in total shock and Lacey pulled her from the room.

Penny turned to everyone and said, "No more murders around Jim now. Understood?"

Everyone burst out laughing and Penny couldn't hold it either. She turned to me and said, "That woman was part of a troupe of geeks performing at the Harmon Theatre. I talked her into coming here to purge you of your curse. Now, I insist that you stop killing people."

"For you, anything to prevent that from happening again," I said with a sigh of relief.

*

Chapter 24

I thought back on all the times that Penny brought silly things to our home from her talk show back in Michigan. I was always on edge when I would walk in the house, not knowing what to expect, this topped them all and she included our friends.

"You know, I could have had a heart attack when that woman yelled in my face," I said.

"You loved every minute of it, I can tell. Now you aren't going to have any more murder following you. I think she scared that part out of you."

"Oh yes, she did." I said and looked to everyone still in my office. "Don't you people have work to do?"

Trapper laughed. "Just wanted to see the look on your face. I wish I had a camera when that woman walked in."

"Well, it's good you didn't. Now, everyone out of my office, except Penny. I have a few words to say to her."

They all left and Penny came over to me. "You have something to say to me?"

I reached over and grabbed her wrist and pulled her to me. She plopped down on my lap and then put her arms around me and said, "It's good you had an office built for Lynn, so you have your office back all to yourself.

I reached over to the phone on my desk and pushed a button to signal Lacey. She answered.

"Lacey, do not disturb me, and I mean it."

"Fine. Just keep the noise down in there." Lacey said and laughed. I turned off the phone.

~~*~~

Deacon's cell phone buzzed and he answered after looking at the caller ID. It was Greg Warren. "Greg, what do you have?" Deacon hit the speaker button so Buck could hear.

"The perp has landed." Warren said.

"Where?"

"South Bermuda, just below Warm Springs, behind Vegas Premium Outlet. It's a small building, like an office building. There were four cars around it. The perp just drove in and went inside."

"Great, text me the address and I'll get a search warrant." Deacon stood and went out of his office to Captain Weber's office. He knew Weber could get a warrant faster than he could. He knocked at Weber's door and went in when invited. He explained the situation and Weber got on his phone.

"Get out there and I'll have the warrant delivered. Good work, DeAngelo."

"I've got good people," he said and left the office.

Buck was standing just outside Deacon's office when Deacon came back into the squad room. He called to the men in the room. "Listen up! If you're not working on something important, I need a posse to go to the place where the missing dogs may be. And hopefully we'll find our killers. Tyler, I'll text you the address, call SWAT and get them organized. Everyone else, follow me."

Deacon and Buck went out the back door to the motor pool. Deacon signed out the Dodge Charger Interceptor and got in. Buck jumped in the passenger seat and they went off. Four cop cars were streaming south to Warm Springs with sirens blaring. Deacon radioed a 'go silent' order to the other cars as they approached the location. They turned south on Bermuda and Deacon saw Warren's car parked on the street. He pulled up behind it and exited the car.

"Are they still inside?" Deacon asked.

"Nobody's come out. I presume there are more than one person inside. There are five cars out front of the building, so figure at least five people inside," Warren replied.

"Okay, until the warrant arrives along with SWAT, we just sit tight. If anyone leaves the building, I'll have a car follow."

They stood watching the building and waiting. About twenty minutes later, the warrant came with the SWAT captain. Deacon and the captain organized the attack and then they went towards the side of the building with less windows.

Deacon tried a door and it wasn't locked. He opened it and stuck his head in, listening. He could hear dogs barking in the distance and smiled. "Well, we may just tie this all up."

Deacon signaled and everyone streamed into the building. They raced down a hallway, checking doors along the way. The rooms behind the doors were all empty. Deacon could hear dogs barking at the end of the hall. He signaled to the captain of the SWAT and they went to the door. The captain listened and reached for the door knob. It turned and opened. The SWAT men shot into the room. It was a large garage, with double garage doors opening to the back of the building. One door was open and a van was parked just outside. There were two men at the van while three more were at the dog cages. They looked to be transferring the animals into boxes.

"Freeze!" Deacon yelled as the police surround the men. The two men outside by the van started to run off, but Deacon thought to have men stay outside and they stopped the fleeing men.

The men in the room didn't put up a fight, they all surrendered. "That's the way I like a take down to go. No bullets used." Deacon said to Buck.

"That should please Weber," Buck said with a laugh.

Kennel Murders

Deacon handed Buck his list of dogs from the murder scene kennel. "Check this list and your list to see if the dogs are all here."

"Gotcha," Buck said and went to take inventory of the animals.

All the men were rounded up and cuffed. Deacon walked down the line of men, watching their eyes. Two looked down and the rest gave Deacon an evil stare. "I want to talk to you and you," he said pointing to the two men who looked way. The officer with the keys released the two and then re-cuffed them to each other. Deacon pulled the men out of the line and into a small room off the side of the garage.

"Okay, guys, you two don't seem to have the stomach for this. You can get a lighter sentence if you cooperate. I need to know who the power behind this is. The head man, or woman. If you want to skate on murder charges, talk to me."

Both men got a frightened look on their faces. They looked at each other and nodded.

"Can you keep us out of this if was give up the leader?" one of the men asked.

"We'll do our best. Now, who is the person in charge?"

"I don't know his name but he comes in here with his dog. A Labrador Retriever named Sandy. I've heard him call to the dog when it went to the cages to nose the other dogs."

Deacon looked shocked. He tried to remember back to the day in the convention center. The man who identified the thief who took the show dog. He said his dog, a Labrador Retriever, was named Sandy. Ray Zink.

Deacon went to the door and called Buck and Warren. They came in and Buck said "All but two dogs are here."

"Doesn't matter now. We have another problem. The boss man of this operation is Ray Zink. Our friendly identifier of the show dog grab."

*

Chapter 25

Penny was straightening out her clothes as she left my office. She turned and said, "Don't get up, I can find my way." She laughed aloud and went to the front.

"Do you feel like going shopping?" Penny asked Lacey as she entered the front lobby.

That took Lacey by surprise. "What's the occasion?"

"I just charged Jim two hundred dollars for making out. I want to spend it before he takes it back."

"You charge your husband to make out?"

"Only when I want to go shopping."

"Okay, let me tell Tracey that I'm going." Lacey went out the outer lobby and brought Tracey back into the inner lobby.

"Willy!" Penny called. The dog came running out of the hallway and Penny picked him up. She then put him in his purse and told Lacey to follow.

The two of them went out to Penny's car and drove off.

Between the two of them, they decided to go to the Boulevard Mall. About twenty minutes later they arrived. Penny decided to use the valet parking and the two of them went in the front entrance.

"What are you interested in buying?" Lacey asked.

"Let's start at the jewelry stores."

~~*~~

Deacon stood in the center of the garage and said to Buck. "All these men are going back to be interrogated. Just to see if their stories jive. Now we have to find Zink."

"Valstad said he boarded his dog with her once, so she should have his address." Buck said.

"Can you call her and ask? Don't mention about us finding these dogs yet. I don't want her giving anything away." Deacon said, then added, "See if we have the Lawson's dog in this mess, so we can let him know."

Kennel Murders

"I already checked and there are two dogs still missing. Lawson's was one of them. At least both of the dogs that were taken at the dog show are here."

"Well, this should make a number of people happy. I'll have Warren start contacting the owners to come and get their pets. Go call Valstad."

"Will do, be right back." Buck went to the outside of the garage where it was quiet—no dogs barking to give anything away. He called her and told her he needed Zink's address to get him to identify the man killed behind the pet store. It was a good excuse and Valstad gave him the info. He said he had to go and hung up before she could ask any more questions.

Buck came back to Deacon and gave him the address. He called to a couple detectives and officers who were just standing around. "Guys, let's roll. Got a new suspect to detain." Then he turned to Warren, "Greg, take over here and see the dog all get home."

Warren agreed as Deacon, Buck and the men went out. They got to their cars as Deacon checked the address. It was up by Jim and Penny's home. He smiled and looked at Buck, "Well, this will make Jim real happy to have a dog theft kingpin in his backyard."

They drove out and over to the address about a half mile from Jim and Penny's house. They all pulled up to the house, five cars all coming to a stop on the road and in the drive. There was a Ford Bronco parked in front of the garage.

Everyone spread out as Deacon organized the attack. He went up to the front door and banged, yelling "Police, Mr. Zink, open up."

A minute later the door opened and Zink stood there looking mildly surprised. "I didn't think you'd find me so fast. Good work gentlemen. Come in please."

Deacon was puzzled by this new development. He entered, followed by two of his men, with Buck heading up the rear.

"You're Detective DeAngelo, correct?"

Deacon agreed.

"Come into the living room and we can talk." He walked into the rather spacious, well decorated room. Everyone followed, keeping a watchful eye on Zink.

Deacon turned to one of his officers and said to tell the others outside to wait. The officer went off, following command. Deacon turned to Zink and asked, "Where's your Labrador?"

"Oh, I gave her to my ex-wife to watch for me. I figured you'd be coming soon enough. I didn't want to leave Sandy all alone."

"Why did you figure we were going to find you?" Deacon asked.

"After I deliberately gave you the description of Karl Hotchkiss, I knew you'd find him. I hadn't counted on him being killed behind the pet shop by my men, but he did try to cheat us out of a ransom for that dog."

"Why did you deliberately give us the description of Hotchkiss?"

"To throw you off from me. I messed up when your people found me in the kennel the other day. I shouldn't have been there. I was sure it made you suspect me."

Deacon didn't want to admit the thought hadn't really crossed his mind. "We only had it substantiated by one of your men at the office building on Bermuda."

"Ah, yes. But I'll tell you it's not my building."

"What's that mean?"

"I'm not the person in charge of this operation here in Vegas. I did bring my men here from LA at the request of a local dog lover, and someone who wanted a lot of quick money. My dog theft ring in LA was wearing a little thin, we were on a police watch. We had to move, and were given the opportunity here."

"Who gave you that opportunity?"

"You don't know? I'd have thought you would have figured it out. Cindy Valstad hired us."

Deacon was shocked. "Valstad? But she was robbed of dogs too."

"Oh, come on. She knew the right dogs to take. She marked the cards on the cages of the really expensive dogs to steal. Some of my men got greedy and went to the other kennel to steal more dogs, but they were interrupted. That man died for being in the wrong place. Such a shame. I don't approve of murder."

Deacon asked, "There are still two dogs missing, where are they?"

"Valstad has them. I called the Lawsons about the ransom, but they didn't answer their phone. I figured that had something to do with you. Valstad was going to return the dogs after the ransom was paid. She was going to say some man dropped off the dogs."

"You're being awful cooperative about this."

"I have good lawyers and I didn't do anything other than bring my men here. Valstad made all the deals and gave all the orders. I'll get off like I did in LA every time I got pinched."

Deacon turned to one officer and said, "Cuff him, read him his rights, and take him in." He turned to Buck, "Let's go nab a ring leader."

They left and Deacon called for back-up at the kennel, just in case.

Buck said, "I can't believe that nice lady was behind all this."

"Yeah, Ma Barker seemed like a nice lady until she started shooting people."

"I don't think she'll be shooting anyone."

"I never count on anything to go as it seems. Just be ready to duck."

About ten minutes later they came to the Happy Puppy Kennel and pulled to the rear of the building.

Everyone was ready to go in. Deacon said, "Hold here, I'm taking Buck in the front to assess the situation."

*

Chapter 26

"Are you going to stand behind me in case she starts shooting?" Buck asked as they walked up the side of the building to the front entrance.

Deacon laughed and said, "No, she knows you so she may not suspect anything."

"Damn, she hired me to find the dognappers. Now that we know she's the leader, I wonder if I'll get paid."

Deacon laughed again and said, "You didn't get a retainer? Shame on you."

They got to the front door and went in. There was no one at the front counter. Deacon whispered, "Does she have cameras?"

"No, I found that out when I first started investigating this place."

Deacon reached over to that bell on the counter and pushed the lever. It rang loudly. They waited.

Suddenly, the curtains to the back parted and out came Lori, the girl who gave the thieves info about the dogs at the private homes. She seemed surprised. "Detective, are you here to talk to me?"

"No, Lori, is Ms. Valstad in?" Deacon asked the girl.

"She's busy in the back. Do you really have to talk to her?"

"I'm afraid so." Deacon said as he moved around the counter to the door to the back. Buck was right behind him. They broke through the curtains to find Valstad on the side of the room tied to a chair.

"What the hell," Deacon said as he and Buck went to her. Deacon reached over and pulled the gag from her mouth.

"Behind you," Valstad said, weakly.

Deacon and Buck turned to see Lori with a short barreled shotgun aimed at them. "You just couldn't wait until I got the last of the ransoms," she said.

"No one is paying the ransom, we got all the dogs." Deacon said.

"No, these two are still being ransomed and they are the most valuable ones." She pointed to the last two dogs in cages. "I finally got through to the Lawsons and they agreed to pay the ransom. And to the Eliots, they agreed to pay also. I just needed another half hour to get the funds transferred. I'm not totally heartless. I was going to give them their dogs back. By the time they figured it out, I was going to be far away from here."

"How does Valstad figure into this?"

"She's just the owner of this kennel, she never knew what was going on. She won't tell anyone after I kill her, I'll make sure she'll take the blame."

"Maybe so, but what about us?" Deacon asked.

She was silent then said, "Okay, I'll shoot you two with the shotgun and then kill Valstad with your gun. I can say it was a gun fight with her. I'll tell everyone she was the person in charge."

"Wait, before you kill us, why did Zink identify Valstad as the leader of this operation?" Deacon asked.

"I guess it will be all right to tell you, since you are a dead man. He's my father, and he'd never turn me in. I came out here with him from LA to get a job here to establish a base of operations. Dad arranged it all."

Deacon looked at Buck, "Well, this changes things."

"Changes what?" Lori asked.

"How we're going to explain to the prosecutor about this mess."

"You're not going to tell anyone about this, because you'll be dead," she said, just as a hand reached around her and grabbed the shotgun and pulled it up. She screamed as she turned to see the cop standing behind her, now holding the shotgun.

Deacon and Buck both rushed and subdued her. She was kicking and screaming, but they held her tight until they could get the cuffs on her.

A number of cops came into the room. Deacon said, "I'm glad you guys don't follow orders."

"We got antsy out back. Decided to join the party." The cop holding the shotgun said.

The other officers took Lori out as Deacon said to be sure to read her the Miranda rights.

They went to untie Valstad and helped her up. She said she was a bit dizzy.

"Lori gave me some drink that she said was healthy. I guess it wasn't," she said.

"We came here to arrest you for this mess." Deacon said.

"You need to call the Lawsons and the Eliots and tell them not to transfer their money." Valstad said.

Deacon got on his cellphone to call Warren. He hung up and said, "My man will take care of it. Are you all right?"

"I need to sit down, but I think I'll be all right."

An hour later, the Lawsons and the Eliots came to get their dogs. Valstad was resting in the front as everyone was moving around doing their thing.

"What's going to happen to Lori?" She asked Buck as he rested by the counter.

"Probably a long time in prison, especially with murder charges for Hotchkiss and the kennel employee hanging over her. Accessory to murder, I think they call it. And don't forget attempted murder on you, me and Deacon."

"Shame, she was my best employee."

"Maybe you'll ask for better references next time," Buck said with a smile.

"Thank you, Mr. Carson. I'll have a check made out to your firm this week."

"All in a day's work," he said.

Deacon came up and told Valstad that she would need to give her statement at the precinct tomorrow, then he said they were finished there and he went out, followed by Buck.

~~*~~

Lynn came into the office just as Penny and Lacey entered before her. I came rolling out from behind the lobby counter and said. "Nice of everyone to get back to work. I talked to Buck a little while ago and he said they wrapped up the dognapping ring."

Tracey was giggling behind the counter. Penny came up and said, "Have you been telling Tracey jokes again?"

"I was keeping her occupied. What did you buy?"

"Never mind. Talk to us about the dognappers." Penny said.

I covered as much as Buck told me. Then I said, "I'm sure Deacon will have more to say about it."

I spun my chair to Lynn and said, "Where have you been hiding out?"

"I was spending some quality time with my daughter. I was getting tired of dogs."

"You're not a dog owner. I should let you take care of Willy for a week and you'll come around."

"No thank you, I change enough stinky stuff without having to clean up after a dog."

The front door opened and Deacon came in with Buck. Deacon went straight for Lynn and gave her a hug. Buck said he had to work on his report of the dog case, looking at Lacey, then he went to his office.

"If Earl and Trapper were here we could have a party," I said.

Penny came over to me, "Do we really need them to party?"

"I guess not," I said and turned my chair towards the door to the lounge. "I'm going to start my own party, anyone care to join me?"

*

The End.

For every ending, there's a new beginning.

Bob Moats

Here's a free preview of the next book "Trick or Treat Murders"

Chapter 1

HALLOWEEN – 1999

The doorbell rang twice before the woman opened the door. She lived on a lonely stretch of road, so she was mildly surprised that there was a trick-or-treater pushing her doorbell. Her porch light was on—to signify there was candy—so she could see the creature standing alone at her door. The person, boy or girl, hard to tell she thought, stood fairly tall. She wondered if it was an over-sized child or some teenager begging for treats.

"Trick or Treat," came a voice from under the small, dirty-looking, burlap bag covering the head and tied around the person's neck. There were two small holes cut for eyes and the woman could see very dark brown, almost black, eyes from within the recesses. It was hard to tell if the voice came from a girl, or a boy just before puberty. It was high pitched and yet sounded rough.

The woman studied the costume, mostly homemade, so she assumed the person was not very well off monetarily. Other than the bag covering the head, the person wore a plaid wool shirt, like a lumberjack wore, and baggy blue jeans. She noticed the person had no shoes or socks. This disturbed her as it was fairly cold for Halloween in the Vegas Valley.

"You need shoes more than candy," the woman finally said.

The person just stood waiting.

"Well, I guess if it doesn't bother you, it's none of my business."

"No, it isn't, Mrs. Hall," the bag spoke.

That shook the woman up, the person knew her name. How? Was the person a neighbor or someone from her church?

"None of your business at all, Mrs. Hall," the bag spoke again. "You don't remember where my shoes are, do you?"

"Excuse me? I don't know who you are with that bag on your head. So how would I know where your shoes are?"

"Of course you wouldn't remember accusing me of stealing Jeffery's shoes, would you?" The voice was now more threatening, almost growling. "You made me give them back to that dirty little liar."

A chill ran through the woman, hearing the menace in the voice. She searched her mind to try to remember accusing anyone of stealing anyone's shoes. She vaguely remembered her long dead son had taken a friend's shoes and she made him give them back. But this person couldn't be her son. He died a few years back from an attack by an unknown assailant and left in a drainage canal. Blow to the head the police said. She had a hard time identifying the body, it had been in water for a week. But the clothes and a wallet did help identify the boy.

"Who are you and why are you saying these things?" The woman was starting to panic. "Go away, I have no candy for you!"

"Wait, Mrs. Hall. I have to give you your trick." The person reached into the bag, pulled out a .38 handgun, and fired it into the woman's chest in a perfect shot grouping.

The woman's face contorted in shock and pain as she fell back onto the rug in the hallway. The hooded assailant put the gun back into the bag and said, "Trick or treat, Mom."

PRESENT DAY - 2013

"Now how do they know the killer said that?" I asked while sitting at my desk in my office listening to Deacon tell the story.

Deacon smiled and said. "The whole incident was caught on camera. The woman's husband was a security freak. He had cameras everywhere around the house. Luckily, they also recorded sound. The whole thing was recorded so we knew what had happened. The case was never solved, lack of evidence left at the scene."

"So, you're saying the woman's son came back from the dead to take revenge for the incident with the shoes?"

"I didn't say that. I don't believe in ghosts or zombies," he said crossing himself.

"Why did you just do that?"

"Jim, I was raised in an Italian and devout Catholic home. It's an old habit when talking about the dead." Deacon smiled.

"But you said you didn't believe in ghosts or zombies, they're undead."

"The victims we have to face when we go out on a murder case are usually dead. I sometimes cross myself depending on who the vic is."

"Whatever, now back to the Trick-or-Treat Killer. There was no evidence to point to the perp?"

"Nope. Everything the recording revealed was never substantiated by the husband. He never heard about any shoe incident. He did say he couldn't identify his son's body. Too badly decomposed."

"You're thinking it might not be the son who died. That the son murdered some boy and dressed him up in his own clothes and left evidence that the body was the son. Am I right?"

"This is why I like you, Jim. You have a devious mind that gets to the point. Most times."

"Most times? When have I been wrong?" I protested.

"You really want me to list them?" he said with a grin.

I shut up.

Kennel Murders

"Halloween is in four days. Every year for the last fourteen, a woman has been shot at her door by an unknown assailant. The link between all those murders is that ballistics showed it was the same gun as the first killing."

"So this bag wearing, gun-toting, killer is celebrating Halloween by shooting women? Why haven't I heard warnings about this? I'm surprised that the city fathers haven't banned trick-or-treating."

"Oh, they talked about it, but Halloween in Vegas isn't something they can control. LVPD puts out more cars on the streets, but we don't have enough men to cover every street in the city. They did issue warnings on all the news stations, but that one murder always slips through."

"Same gun every year, huh? How many moms does this dead boy have?" I asked.

"We haven't been able to find a connection between all the dead women, except they've all been murdered on Halloween. None of them knew each other, they didn't go to the same church, nor were they in any social clubs together. A couple of them had gambling problems, but that's hardly a cause to murder them. So, we are on high alert to keep one woman from dying this year, as we have been for the last twelve years, when we realized the pattern of the crimes."

"Well, I don't envy you this job. With thousands of people walking around in disguises, how do you land one bad guy, or ghost? Maybe you can call those paranormal ghost hunters from the TV." I chuckled.

"That suggestion got laughed down two years ago. We don't even bring it up anymore. It's believed that the original killer is still doing this every year. If he was the boy who the Halls said was their dead son, he'd be around twenty-eight now. I believe that's what happened, he's still out there."

"Well, if he's killing in Vegas, then he must still live here. I'd say he was a very patient serial killer. Are you going to let a fourteen year murder spree go without an investigation?"

"I was hoping you'd say that," Deacon said with a big grin.

"Oh, sure, stick this on me. Your people couldn't investigate their way out of a paper bag. Besides, I just got out of a leg cast and I'm barely able to walk straight and you want me to investigate a creepy dead kid murdering his mother over and over."

"I knew you'd love the idea."

I sat staring at my friend. "I'll need to see the original recording of the first kill."

Kennel Murders

Deacon handed me a flashdrive. I laughed, "You were pretty sure of yourself."

He smiled and said, "I read you like one of your books."

*

Continued in the book....

~~*~~

Bob Moats

Jim Richards Family of Readers

Thanks to the following people who are now part of the Jim Richards Family of Readers. They have read a book or more and enjoyed them. They all volunteered to be included in the list. If you are a fan of the books, send me your full name and you will be included in future books. Send your name to murdernovels@bobmoats.com to be added here and on the website. (Updated 3-29-14)

* Achim Feifel * Al Norris * Alex Wheatley * Alexandra Delporte-Wilkinson * Amy Tapia * Andrea Bryan * Anne Shepherd * Arianda Sugar * Arlene Markowski * Ashley Augustus * Audra Hall * Barbara Hughes * Barbara Sammons * Barbara Schuler * Barbara Zirger * Beth Donohue Plenskofski * Betsy Childress * Beth Gibson * Bill Sandy * Bill Tornquist * Billie-jo Collie * Boni J Rychener * Carl Bishopric * Carla Lewis * Carole Henderson * Carolyn Conroy * Carolyn Riddle-Linington * Cassy Bailey * Chad Hudson * Charlotte L Duran * Cheryl L. Everett * Cindy Ackley Nunn * Cindy Valstad * Connie Bancroft * Corinne Kay O'Daniel * Dana Robbins Chuchran * Dana Wichita * Danielle Monique * Darren Heald * Dave Travers * David Wilkinson * DeAnn Jannereth * Deanna Miller * Deb Breuker Balbo * Debbie Carter * Debbie White * Deborah Fartuch * Deborah Gauze * Deborah Sullivan * Dee King * Denise Freeman * Diana Carver * Dixie Beck * Donna Gould * Donna Thompson * Donny Minter * Doris Kight * Eddie Moore

Kennel Murders

* Eric Walters * Felicia Annette Bradfield * Francine Menor * Gail Chesney * Georgiann Minster * George Conner * Greg Colucci * Hayley Rankin * Harold Garcia * Heidi Arnold * Irma Ranee Coy * Jacqueline Moss * Jan Kimball * Janice Schneider * Janice Spoor * Jennifer Redmond * Jessica Keown-Belous * Jim Beck * Jo Boguslaw * Jo Turner * Joanne Marie Turner * John Peiffer * John Wisbiski * Joseph Wauro * Joyce Stacy * Joyce Trifiletti * Judy Franklin * Judy Travers * Judy Padgett * Julie Heath * Junnahvee Benson * Karen Dahl * Karen Grams * Karen Higham * Karen Kaiser * Karen Meinburg Richwine * Karen Kirkman Parker * Karin Hawkins * Karin Vasvari * Kathleen Donohue Roesing * Kathleen Riddle-Wolfe * Kathy Hinds Moore * Kathy Jones * Kathy Mitchell * Katie Benzler * Kay Burns * Kelly Garcia * Ken Boggs * Keota Rodriguez * Kiera Mccarthy * Kim Estes * Kitty Stolle * Kristie Sciler * Kirsty Stanton * LaLonnie Scallen * Larry Morris * Leann Parr * Lenora Scales * Leslie Marie Jackson * Linda Forester * Linda Ingle Cox * Linda Kennerö * Linda Magill * Lisa Bower * Liz Gibson * Lorraine Wiman * Loretta Alexander * Lynda Bowles * Lynette Lawrance * LuAnn Louttit * Manny Rothman * Marcia Gibson DeWitt * Marie Calder * Marlene Bryan * MaryLouise Kramp * Mary Lynn Gross * Megan Atkins * Meghan Hyden * Melody Cannavan * Michael Carruthers * Michael Dinkens * Michael Vannoy * Michelle Burns-Mitchell * Michelle Pilcher * Micki Potter * Mike Moats * Mimi Baur * Myrna Hecht * Nadine Sutton * Natalie Quine * Neena Martin * O'Della Wilson * Pat Pollington * Pat Rohn * Patricia Jarmon * Patricia C Trezza * Patrick Barry * Paul Lawrance * Peggy Davis * Phyllis Bassett * Raylene Matheny * Rebecca Collins Besner * Renee Brumley * Reta Hanna * Reta Moats * Roberta Navarro-Harder * Sally Berneathy * Sally Hubler * Sarah Santos *

Bob Moats

Satka Nikc * Sharon E. Edwards * Sharon Mangini * Sharon McMillon * Sheena Rawl * Sherry Amstutz * Shirley Alvarez * Shirley Davies * Shirley Williams * Stacie Rowe * Stephanie Conner * Steve Cullen * Susan Haughton * Susan Hesse Adams * Susan Salomon * Suzan K Chase * Taisha Cullum * Tamara Moore * Tammy Castleberry * Tammy Lynn Wood * Ted Murphy * Terri Atkins * Terri Creech * Terry Raab * Tonia Rachael Riggs-Williams * Travis Fleury-Lopez * Twyla Gawlas * Val Brooks * Walt Munsel * Yvonne Isakson *

Thank you to all these wonderful people.

Thank you for purchasing this book. I hope you enjoy it as much as I enjoyed writing it for my faithful readers. Please feel free to email me to tell me what you thought about my stories. I love hearing from the readers. I can be reached at murdernovels@bobmoats.com thanks again!

*